A PROPER
HOLIDAY

ANN OAKLEY

A PROPER
HOLIDAY

Flamingo
An Imprint of HarperCollinsPublishers

Flamingo
An Imprint of HarperCollins*Publishers*
77–85 Fulham Palace Road,
Hammersmith, London W6 8JB

Published by Flamingo 1996
9 8 7 6 5 4 3 2 1

First published in Great Britain by
HarperCollins*Publishers* 1996

ISBN 0 00 655014 2

Set in Bembo

Printed and bound in Great Britain by
Caledonian International Book Manufacturing Ltd, Glasgow

To the Real Youth Club,
and especially Laura and Holly

CONTENTS

1 The Woman in the Golden Bikini   1

2 Mud   15

3 Sweet Sixteen   40

4 Turtle Beach   69

5 The Night of the Storm   84

6 Freedom and Desire   111

7 Postcards Home   125

8 Master-riders in the Realm of Bliss   141

9 The Rubbish Heap of Knowledge   162

10 Jade's Dream   180

11 The Maid's Story   191

12 Fly and Smile   204

ONE

The Woman in the Golden Bikini

Crispin Delancey raised his head from his sunbed and turned it slightly to look at the woman who was about to lower herself into the aquamarine pool. The effort was painful. He was lying on his stomach, which was not quite what it had once been, and muscles buried beneath the layers of untanned flesh twanged uncomfortably when he tried to call them into service.

She was thirty-ish, he supposed. Her compact body wore a yellow bikini like a second skin. She had light, crinkly hair which sparkled in the sharp mid-morning sunlight, creating altogether the appearance of a svelte, illuminated lemon. Crispin watched her as she swam proficiently across the circular pool. He didn't recollect seeing her at the airport yesterday, but then there'd been several busloads of them destined for different hotels.

'You'll burn if you don't do something about it!' A large tapestry bag arrived by Crispin's right ear accompanied by his fun-loving, fattish, forty-something wife, Dodo. 'Remember last year? You looked like a beetroot. And it's worse now, because of the ozone layer.'

Crispin turned over, sat up, and squinted at the sun on its busy skin-damaging journey across the sky. 'Okay, where's the stuff, then?'

'You always rely on me, don't you?' grumbled Dodo happily. She reached into the depths of her very large tapestry bag, wherein suncreams nestled with Mary Wesleys and Fay Weldons, and packets of sweets and plasters and aspirin and tissues and Jacob's cream crackers, and a copy of the insurance document which told them how to get flown home in the event of broken legs and other emergencies. 'There you are, you can start with a factor twenty. I'd better do your back for you.'

Dodo's hands pounded his flesh with thin almond-scented cream, and her mouth rattled words, wrapped in the same aroma, towards him. 'The girls have gone off to inspect the village. They're convinced there's a disco in it somewhere. Can you remember what the man in the travel agent's said? That rep for the travel company – the one who met us at the airport yesterday – she's supposed to be coming here today. We should ask her about going to Ephesus. It'd be good for the girls to have a bit of culture. There,' she gave his creamy back one last slap, 'you'll do for a bit.'

Crispin lay down again. It was nice to get away from everything. They always spent two or three weeks abroad in the summer – Dodo claimed a spell in the sun was essential to her survival. He wasn't sure about his. Somewhere in his head he fantasized about a real holiday – one without obligations, without routines, in which one was absolutely free to – well, have a holiday. The problem of getting away from everything was that an awful lot of it seemed to come with you.

Beside him, Dodo was arranging herself on her chair. She'd brought her little clock with her – her sun clock, she called it. It had a timer which pinged when the relevant bits of her had been adequately toasted. He sighed and moved his arms under his head.

'You all right, darling? Later, when the rep comes, we could have a drink.'

That was another thing about a holiday – all that eating and drinking. You came away for the sake of your health, but if you didn't go home looking healthy, which meant brown, people made you feel guilty about it, though nowadays if you did look brown, there were other people who went on about skin cancer, so you couldn't win. Maybe he should read something, get his brain into gear. But like the muscles in his stomach, the cells in Crispin's brain twanged painfully at the very idea. It had been a hard year. The recession, like the ozone layer, was really biting. Delancey Designs was doing okay, but Crispin was having to work harder at it than a few years ago. The move to the new building, a warehouse in Camden converted with neat wrought-iron staircases and a lot of black wood and grainy steel fittings, had cost a lot, which Crispin's new executive director, a hard-bodied individual with an MA in marketing from Salford Business School, argued they would soon recoup via a vastly enlarged profit-making profile.

Crispin was a reluctant businessman. He and Dodo had been children of the 1960s. Flower children. Dodo had worn long skirts and Crispin flowered shirts, and they'd stuck flower transfers on their Citroën Dyane: roses and poppies larger and pinker than life and Crispin's own about-to-be-sunburned back. All had been rootless pleasure – music, laughter, love, sex, freewheeling circles of hash smoke – though he had been keener on that than Dodo, who'd always worried that it would make her do something she didn't want to, a possibility that was made more likely in view of the fact that she usually didn't know what she did want.

From then to now: Crispin has problems piecing this journey

together. Though he wears business suits (and fashion has brought bright-coloured shirts back in), though he has an accountant and a solicitor and a bank manager and too many bank accounts, mortgages and loans to list on the fingers of both hands, and though he and Dodo live in fashionable Hampstead in a married, nuclear family kind of way, though he is a father and attends PTA meetings to protest against the education cuts, and is a member of the local Residents' Association to protest about the residents' parking scheme and the bumps in the roads, yet it is still possible that at heart Crispin Delancey remains an unrepentant flower child.

Later, when the representative from the Proper Holiday travel company came, they all sat round the bar by the side of the pool. Next to Dodo was the woman with the nice body in the golden bikini. Crispin tried smiling at her slightly while the state of his face still allowed him to do so in comfort. Next to golden bikini was a tall man, brown and furry as a monkey, wearing a peaked cap and a brass chain. Peaked cap man had lost his mother, apparently, and someone else, more credibly, a child. The Delanceys' own offspring, Jade, aged sixteen, and Star, aged fifteen, strode towards the bar from the direction of the town with the sun striking the metal eyelets of their DMs and glancing off their purple (Jade) and black (Star) hair, though only Jade's had multi-coloured extensions in it (£16 a time from Here's Hair in Hampstead High Street).

Carly Atkins from Proper Holidays cleared her throat and welcomes them – but she'd done that already, yesterday, at Karaman airport, when she'd made her usual weak jokes about the airport being a military installation, and the absence of signs being intentional, like in Britain during the war and as portrayed in the currently replaying TV series *Dad's Army*

4

which Carly's mum had given her on a video for Christmas. Carly apologized for her voice, which was croaky. She had a throat infection, and had been run down ever since breaking off her liaison with the Ocakkoy rep, a pedantic ex-geography teacher with a bowel problem. She offered them all drinks. Peaked cap ordered a beer, so did Crispin (might as well). Dodo had a mineral water; golden bikini a glass of white wine. An elderly man with half-moon glasses and grey woollen socks strapped in Clarks sandals below knee-length khaki shorts had a Turkish coffee. A woman who came out of the shade of the big umbrella by the river in a brilliant white and yellow tent dress with glasses on a chain round her neck and a face like shortcrust pastry asked for an *ayran*, the local yoghurt drink.

Carly had lists of points to run through. Her croaky voice has the timbre of a 78 r.p.m. gramophone record while she did it. Information about the hotel (who spoke English, what to do if there was a problem); about the immediate environs – which way the river ran to the sea, what to look at in Karput, which restaurants to avoid and which to patronize (especially the Dircan, with whose young and soulful owner Carly might go to the beach on her next day off). Peaked cap man was worried about the food, or rather about the food in relation to his mother (still absent). Peaked cap man's woman, a small thin-faced brunette with pearly pointed nails and a silver cross round her neck, asked about the safety of the drinking water. Half-moon glasses wanted to know if a day trip to Pamukkale was feasible – he wanted to see Aphrodisias, which according to him was one of the best, but least known, ancient sites, and when Carly said it wasn't, he went on about the Byzantine ruins on the island of Gemile where a sunken village could be glimpsed under the water on a clear day, if you were lucky.

Behind them, a podgy lad bounced a large ball relentlessly on the hot stones. 'Stop that, Stevie!' shouted peaked cap's woman at him. 'Tell him to stop it, Derrick!' Stevie stopped when a little dark-eyed girl with eyes like chocolate buttons came to stand in front of him, quietly watching.

'Oh there you are, Primrose! I'm sorry, is this drinks time?' The line of faces at the bar turned to look.

Carly consulted her list. 'Ah, Mr and Mrs Holbeach. Do come and sit down. I'm afraid you've missed a bit, but I'll go on anyway.' She giggled insincerely, breaking into a nasty cough. 'And if any of you want to buy a carpet . . .' Most of them do, and most of them get done by the brigade of quick-witted mathematicians in Karput. Last year a well-known businessman from Docklands who stayed at the luxurious Princess Rosa in Ocakkoy went home with a polyester carpet for which he paid £2000. He could have got the genuine version for half that not a mile from his office.

Carly told them all about the market in Kitayuk to which they might go if at least eight of them wanted to, thus justifying the hire of a minibus. The bus would take them first to Surlyu, which was staffed by Carly's colleague, Iris, who would accompany them to the market and show them where they could buy hand-beaten copper coffee-grinders and rolls of Osborne and Little curtain material for a fraction of the UK price. Dodo asked about Ephesus, the culture of which she was anxious to inflict on her daughters. Jade and Star made sulky heaving noises, saying in unison, 'We're not going to Ephi-bloody-sus. You can go without us. We'll stay here, thank you very much.'

Half-moon spectacles fixed Jade and Star with a distinctly disapproving stare. 'Ephesus is a unique historical site, young ladies,' he told them. 'You would be ill-advised to miss it.'

Jade and Star stared back. 'Well, we'll be ill-advised, then,' remarked Jade.

Carly stopped coughing. 'Yes, well, there's something for everyone in Turkey. Now, for the nature-lovers among you . . .'

Apart from the river at their backs, wide, free-flowing and not too full of the local sewage, there were the beaches at Moybat, great half moons of silver sand to be reached by the *dolmus* (a Turkish word meaning literally 'full up'), or by private boat, where there was snorkelling to be done in historic caves; and on Datya beach there were even the famous turtles, or rather caches of turtle eggs buried at the water's edge and waiting for the full moon to hatch, so that the baby turtles' eyes would catch the light of the moon on the sea and be able to find their way to it. Carly explained how no one was allowed on the beach after eight o'clock at night, in case tourist torches confused the baby turtles with their misdirected brightness. Star Delancey was slightly interested. 'I'd like to see a turtle,' she admitted.

Carly explained that this was unlikely, except in the local information bureau, where a video of turtles hatching could be watched four times daily. 'And then,' she continued cheerfully, 'if you go up the river that way' – she waved a caramel hand towards Karput – 'you come to the mud baths.' She paused for the predictable 'ugh', which wasn't forthcoming. She went on anyway. 'For thousands of years people have believed that mud is good for the skin. You've heard of mud face-packs, haven't you, ladies? Well, the baths here work on the same principle. The mud comes from sulphur springs. It's not a pleasant smell.'

'Ugh!' said peaked cap man's wife at last.

Carly mentioned the non-mud sulphur baths not far from here, and the Turkish baths in Ocakkoy, and the even better ones (run by a friend of Iris's) in Surlyu, and advised the ladies to keep at least some of their clothes on in all of these, and also of course if they went anywhere near a mosque. She told them of the accessibility of the rock tombs that could be seen on the opposite bank of the river. She cautioned against leaving travellers' cheques or credit cards lying around in the hotel, and recommended *ayran* for travellers' tummy. Finally, she told them that this coastal region of Turkey was excellent for bird-watching – Proper Holidays have a regular little stream of Welsh bird-watchers who block-book the west wing of the Rhapsody Palas every year. Crispin had seen a bunch of them earlier, with their bird-like eyes, watching, and their green canvas rucksacks and swinging binoculars like elephants' balls.

He finished his beer and got up to have a pee. 'Derrick Upton,' peaked cap man held his hand over towards Crispin, 'we might as well introduce ourselves as we're holed up here together. And you?'

As Crispin filled Derrick Upton in on names, Jade and Star came over and attached themselves, one to each of his arms, like jellyfish. Both this, and the fact that they were addressing him as 'Daddy', meant that they wanted something. He gave them some money. Derrick Upton watched sympathetically. 'Mine are just the same,' he confided. 'Think you're a bottom-less pit, don't they?'

Jade and Star strode off. 'Hey, where are you going?' Crispin called out after them, as he's supposed to. Jade flicked her purple, extension-streaked hair over her shoulder. The back of her t-shirt, which was black, read 'CRACK SMOKIN' SATAN

WORSHIPPIN' MOTHERFUCKER' in large white letters. 'Don't worry, Daddy, we won't be long.'

When Crispin came back from his pee, Derrick Upton was in the chair next to his with another beer. 'This is the life,' he said, raising his amber glass against the deep blue of the chlorinated pool, 'isn't it! I wonder who that little miss is. Looks a bit out of it, doesn't she!' A serious pre-adolescent stood on the grass by the pool watching Stevie Upton with his ball and Primrose Holbeach watching him. 'Probably belongs to that oddball with glasses and the wife who looks like a tent. Bit serious for this, don't you think? We came because it's cheap. Cheap and cheerful. We went to Sorrento last year. A beer costs four pounds there – it's ten pee here. And you?'

Crispin was saved from answering this one, as Lisa Upton sat down and lit a cigarette on the other side of Derrick. 'Kelly's got a headache.'

'What, already?'

'You know she doesn't like the heat. It'll be prickly heat rash next. Can I have a drink, Derrick?'

'Where's Mum?'

'Sitting in reception reading the *Mail on Sunday*.'

'Where the hell did she get hold of that?'

'No idea.'

'It's not that easy, you know,' reflected Derrick out loud, and Crispin supposed in some way to him, 'taking your mother on holiday. But what else can I do? She wouldn't get away otherwise. Of course, when the kids were younger, she came in useful for babysitting, but it'll soon be the other way around.'

Crispin saw golden bikini again at lunch, for which they sat at long tables under a raffia awning by the river. She was sitting with a boy of about fifteen or sixteen. The boy ordered a hamburger, she a salad. They ate in what looked to Crispin enviably like a companionable silence. Afterwards the boy got a map out and they studied it together.

At the Delanceys' table, Star picked at a piece of the hard white bread, and Jade squeezed a mound of tomato ketchup over her chips. 'Not everyone here has to be a nuke,' she commented, noting her father's absorption in the scene at the other table. 'Don't stare, Dad, it's rude.'

'Nuke?'

'Nuclear family.'

'Oh.'

'What shall we do this afternoon?' asked Dodo brightly. 'How about a spot of rock climbing? Or snorkelling?'

The girls groaned. 'We've only just got here.'

'I think I'll have a sleep,' said Crispin, 'if you don't mind.'

The Rhapsody Palas had only thirty rooms, built in an L-shape round the circular pool. All the rooms had little patios opening either on to the pool or on to the river. Crispin and Dodo's room opened on to the river, but tall reeds hid it from view. In front of the reeds Suleyman, the hotel gardener, had planted some carmine pink miniature roses called 'Angela Rippon'. The flowers gave weak colour and fragrance to make up for the lack of view and for the incessant noise of the tourist-laden *dolmuses* making their way down river to the sea and the turtles, or up river to the lakes and the mud baths.

The Delanceys' room was like all the others – simply built, with the bed and shelves behind and beside the bed resting on concrete blocks at one with the floor and covered in the same dull-green synthetic carpet. A strip of wood painted the same colour as the carpet ran round the room hiding the electric wiring. In two corners, vertical fluorescent tubes were encased in glass like pickled skeletons in a hospital.

Crispin lay between the cool white sheets listening to the noise of the river boats. There was a slight breeze, so the reeds and the orange-pink and white blooms moved gently between the butterflies and the ordinary flies and the purple-bodied military-looking dragonflies. The door on to the patio was open, but Crispin had drawn the white curtains across it to prevent himself from being seen.

He closed his eyes. The beer had given him a headache. The white curtains waved and voices passed in between the roses. 'If you go to Kas . . . the site of the old theatre . . . binoculars . . . shrub warbler . . . not right . . . how much . . . My wife?' There were two voices, one Turkish and male, one male with another accent. Crispin heard but didn't listen. He was on holiday. Eventually he slept, while the pregnant, potent Euro-Asian air circumnavigated his head, lacing his dreams with exotic enchantments and extraordinary happenings, all delightfully intertwined with the usual flotsam and jetsam of life.

It is before Dodo, and yet after her as well. Crispin is eighteen, a firm youth with the halo of blond curls he has mostly kept – though the halo's thinner now, and merged with grey; then and now it frames Crispin's face with an expression of surprise, like a question mark. In his dream, Crispin is at school, a co-educational boarding school in the green belt. He and his chum Disney Stafford sit in the senior study one summer's evening which is sufficiently warm and aromatic to have been spawned as a memory by his subconscious inhabiting this Turkish hotel now.

The french windows of the study are open to the garden. But instead of the lavender and quiet humming of an English country garden, the window frames vibrant colours. A river, blue like the hotel pool, flows past, carrying a gigantic green turtle on the back of which, like Boadicea, rides the woman in the golden bikini. Her back is straight, her chin raised and the fabric of her bikini shines like liquid gold. She is looking straight ahead and not at him, but Crispin knows she knows he is watching her. For a long moment – no more than a few rapid flickers of the eye in a dream, but in ordinary life one of those instants when the unkind march of time itself is suspended – the trio of Crispin, golden bikini and the turtle are caught there, motionless, trapped in a singular gaze – that of man at woman and woman sensing her existence through being looked at. For the same moment, the turtle enters into the patriarchal conspiracy, but then is called back to its animal origins and shifts in the bright sapphire water, moving man and woman out of the snapped frame of their unequal regard for one another. But as the turtle moves, so Dodo in Crispin's dream enters the study. She is crying. She shouts at him for watching the woman in the golden bikini. While she's shouting, Disney gets up and goes out to the river where the turtle and its rider are still poised, though everything is in motion, like in a film where the landscape is made to rush past artificially, while the principal actors stand still. Disney leaps on to the turtle's back, and they're away: Disney, and the woman in the golden bikini.

Crispin wakes up in a sweat. Someone – in this case Disney – always seems to be one step ahead of him.

Dodo was standing over him holding her bottomless tapestry bag. 'You've been asleep for hours,' she said, accusingly. 'What *were* you dreaming about? I know you were dreaming because you were shouting something. Don't worry, I couldn't make out the words.' She went into the bathroom, still talking. 'It's time to get dressed now. I've arranged to have a drink with some of the others before dinner. Jade and Star seem to be making friends. That's good, isn't it?'

In the village of Karput, the temperature was 32° C. Jade and Star Delancey stood by the toilets attached to the side of the mosque. Jade's posture was intended to be striking, with the sun following the lines of her purple hair, her newly pubertal body and the angles of her hot scuffed boots on the dusty sacred stones. Star was feeding three painfully thin Turkish cats with bread saved from lunch. The two girls were watched by seventeen-year-old Joshua Holbeach, the son of Sandy and Martin Holbeach, who's sitting at a bar across the square with a copy of a magazine called *Black Leather*, drinking neat vodka on ropey ice, and by Kelly and Simon Upton, the elder children of Derrick and Lisa Upton, who had just come out of a shop armed with new dark glasses and postcards for all their friends back home at Chigwell South comprehensive.

'What d'you think, Star?' asked Jade.

'I'll have to come and feed them every day.'

'Not about the cats, stupid. About that boy over there. He's a bit of all right, isn't he?'

Star straightened up. 'He looks like a bit of a poser to me.'

'So what? We've got to find *some* way to pass the time in this place. We're not going bird-watching, are we, and all this toasting oneself is definitely unsound.' You could always tell when Jade was thinking, as she shuffled her feet around and looked down at her boots. 'I wish we were at home.'

'Me too.'

'They'll be going up on the Heath about now.'

'Yes. And then they'll be going to the Metal Ringer.'

'I bet that boy from the hotel has got some hash.'

Joshua Holbeach closed his magazine, got up, and sauntered past the Delancey girls, whistling.

At the bar by the pool, the Rhapsody Palas's head waiter, Kizi Demir, served drinks. Primrose Holbeach and Steven Upton were in the pool still, and Primrose's little brother, Freddie, was floating on it in a blue duck-shaped dinghy. Their mother was leaning over the pool, her third vodka and tonic grasped in a sweaty hand, and wearing a white holiday dress with a lot of cleavage.

Crispin ordered two gin and tonics. 'Local gin or Gordon's?' asks Kizi, with an impeccable accent.

'Oh, local,' said Crispin dreamily.

'I'm not sure that's wise, darling,' hissed Dodo in his ear.

Kizi smiled. It wasn't, but that they must discover for themselves.

Across the river, the sun dropped behind the hillside holding the rock tombs, and the day's last tourists scrambled awkwardly down. Mosquitoes congregate. In the Hotel Rhapsody Palas, waiters lit the anti-mosquito devices, and turned on the pool lights, and the lights in the spindly prickly juniper trees. The wind had dropped. It was breathless.

'Hallo,' she said, 'I'm Meg Shaw. We met earlier.'

TWO

Mud

In the early morning, Meg Shaw and her son, Aaron, sat at one of the raffia-roofed breakfast tables eating rose-fleshed watermelon and planning their expedition to Ephesus. They were going to hire a car – it was ridiculously cheap here, at only £16 plus a driver for the day – and would leave at eight. Unlike the Delancey girls, Aaron Shaw was keen to visit this site, formerly ruled by Croesus, King of Lydia, and to which camel caravans once brought across deserts the colour of his mother's bikini the richly fragranced treasures of the East. At his comprehensive school in a long road joining Shepherd's Bush and Hammersmith in west London there was a history teacher whose enthusiasm for the past was proportional to his disaffection for the present: Bill Griffiths had planted in Aaron the idea that he might want to become an archaeologist.

Aaron was a quiet, thoughtful lad, with a pleasing complexion and light brown hair and eyes. He'd always read a lot and been uninterested in the usual masculine pursuits of sport and noise and violence, which might have been no accident, but had suited Meg quite well, as she found her job as a social worker in the neighbouring district of Acton so taxing that all she wanted was a bit of peace and quiet to come home to. Aaron and Meg had been on their own for fourteen and a half of Aaron's fifteen years. Aaron's father, an extremely peripatetic jazz musician, had never been much interested in social fatherhood and the biological side had been but a brief burst of pleasure, like a firework, or a few bars of *Elite Syncopations*.

Aaron's aim in coming to Turkey was to get a few Greco-Roman ruins under his belt, and Meg's was to get through the pile of books she'd brought with her. Meg wasn't looking for excitement. Since Aaron's father, there had been other men with whom she'd enjoyed flings or more protracted episodes, but all the men had ended up leaving the bay-fronted flat in Bloemfontein Road to the less exacting companionship of mother and son.

Meg got up to refill her coffee cup. The coffee was dreadful – neither Turkish nor French, nor even English. 'There seem to be a lot of young people here,' she commented to Aaron, who was deep in his guide to the Dinacek valley.

'I'm quite capable of finding my own entertainment, Mum.'

Meg worried sometimes about Aaron's lack of sociability, about his immersion in the past rather than the present. 'Have you talked to any of them?'

'What? Would you like to go to Krya, Mum? It has tombs shaped like eagles' nests. Mind you, there's no road, you might not be up to the climb.'

'Don't be rude. I was talking about the other kids here.'

He looked up at her, squinting slightly through the steam of her coffee. 'Leave it out, Mum. They're weird. Those two girls – you know, the ones with DMs – they're called Jade and Star!' He choked with mirth.

'Well, you often complain about your own name.'

'At least it's a real one. They asked me to a nightclub.'

'Is there one?'

'Apparently. It's called "Sweet Sixteen".'

'Well, are you going? Why don't you go with them? You might enjoy it.'

Aaron shook his head in despair, and went back to his guidebook.

While Meg and Aaron Shaw took themselves off in a car to Ephesus, the rest of the Hotel Rhapsody Palas woke up. The Dunkerleys were next – half-moon glasses in Clarks sandals, and woman in a tent dress with a face like pastry. Shortly after the Dunkerleys sat down, a busload of Proper Holiday clients from the early flight arrived for breakfast en route to their self-catering villas in Ocakkoy. So when the Uptons, though not plus Derrick's mum, Wilma Blake, who was having a nice cup of tea in her room, courtesy of a small plastic traveller's kettle purchased at Stansted airport, came to breakfast, there wasn't enough space for them. 'This won't do,' wailed Lisa, stamping her foot. 'We'll have to complain about it. What are we paying all this money for?'

'Shush, dear, we aren't, and I expect they'll be gone soon. Look, there's some space over there with those people we met yesterday.'

Thus were the Dunkerleys and the Uptons forced to make closer acquaintance with one another. Thus, too, young Portia Dunkerley, the Dunkerleys' pre-adolescent daughter, came to sit opposite young Kelly Upton, a position which, leading as it did to a certain sharing of information, could have led to either feeling deprived, though it was in fact Portia who would do so this time. 'D'you wanna come to the beach, then?' offered Kelly, her mouth crammed with the cake-like Turkish bread. 'We could go in one of them boats.' She waved in the direction of Karput harbour. 'It's only five quid to hire one. I've gotta lot of money. How much've you got?'

'Yeah, yeah!' cheered Kelly's thirteen-year-old brother Simon at her elbow. 'There's a fierce bar at the beach.' He frowned at Portia, trying to make her out.

'Thank you for the invitation,' said Ronald Dunkerley on his daughter's behalf, 'but Portia's coming with us today to see the temple and the necropolis at Punka.' (This had been recommended by one of Ronald's colleagues in the history department of the university where he worked. 'Just as good as Ephesus, Dunkerley, but tourist free. Got some decent shade as well. But do watch out for the curse on grave robbers.') 'The temple has a series of interesting unfluted columns,' went on Ronald. 'Never finished, you see, and the necropolis . . .'

'I don't think they're interested in the necropolis or the columns, Daddy,' said Portia quietly.

'Don't she never do nothing on her own?' inquired Kelly.

Portia opened and shut her mouth. 'I'm only twelve,' she came out with eventually.

'So? When I was twelve I did all kindsa things.'

'Are you an archaeologist, Mr Dunkerley?' asked Lisa politely, to divert attention from anything else her daughter Kelly might say.

'It's not "Mr", it's "Professor",' said Portia proudly. 'And my mum's a professor, too!' Not every twelve-year-old had two parents who were professors (or even two parents).

'Well, that's nothing to be proud of,' responded Kelly. 'My mum's a teacher, and my dad's an energy consultant.'

Grizelda Dunkerley peered at Kelly. 'What's an energy consultant?' Grizelda wasn't any good at making conversation. In fact she wasn't very good with words at all, which was strange, as she held the Prudence Kettle Chair in English Literature at the University of the North Midlands. Prudence Kettle had been subject to mystical visions of the millennium rather like those enjoyed by Jane Ward of Norfolk in the 1640s, who'd got out of getting married on the grounds that she was already a bride of Christ, and earthly marriage would be repulsive by comparison. Prudence Kettle had been deemed mad, as visions that were okay in the 1640s were not so in the 1940s, but she'd escaped institutionalization through being the daughter of Lord Creasy of Holkham, spending most of her life in a mansion near there, surrounded by servants and a number of small black dogs.

'Electricity to you,' said Derrick Upton, sipping his over-sweetened cherry juice. 'I do electrical installations. In offices, mostly.' He knew Lisa would attack him after breakfast for owning up to being an electrician. She'd read the term energy consultant in the yellow pages one day when she'd been looking for a music teacher for Stevie. She considered Stevie musical and fancied seeing him with a little violin tucked under his chin. Lisa had more or less given up on her two elder children, though she would have been the last to admit it. Stevie was her last hope. Derrick blamed the influence of the other kids at school himself. He'd caught Lisa looking in the same yellow pages for private schools. 'I'm not having any child of mine educated privately!' There were some things a man had to put his foot down about.

The busload en route to the Ocakkoy villas went, which meant that the Uptons could sit at their own table instead of with the Dunkerleys. 'I'd really like to go to the beach with you one day,' admitted Portia very quickly to Kelly, as though incriminated less by fast words than by slow ones.

Crispin Delancey didn't wake up until Meg Shaw and her quiet son were halfway to Ephesus, the Dunkerleys were approaching Punka with its unfinished unfluted columns, and the Uptons were well entrenched in their marital argument about who was and who was not pretending to be something they weren't. It was Dodo's banging around on the patio erecting a washing line that woke Crispin. At first, he couldn't remember where he was. Then his eyes refocused on the dreadfully blue, dreadfully cloudless sky beyond the window, and the tall reeds shielding the many-boated river. Dodo had a spray of purple bougainvillaea in her hair. She was wearing her new white bikini, bought to show off her suntan, the stigmata of which could just be seen in the form of the criss-cross of yesterday's swimsuit on her back. She seemed about to set off for some more, armed with her pinger and an old Fay Weldon novel about a woman with a low-lying placenta. 'Mustn't waste good sunbathing time,' she announced briskly. 'I've put your towel on the chair next to mine. The girls are asleep, of course. I'm going to wake them up at eleven. Or rather you are. They need a strong father.'

Crispin rolled himself out of bed and took himself off for breakfast. The sun was also horribly bright. He fetched some food and sat down. The river persistently flowed and the purple bougainvillaea persistently bloomed beside him. Thin waitresses in red dresses clashing with the flowers balanced trays with the sun bouncing off their hair. The grass sparkled with newly sprinkled water. Down under the table something moved. Crispin looked. A man was crouching there in a defecating position by a clump of roses. Crispin slid himself and his plate up the table a bit.

'It's only the gardener. They can do things with their bodies we lost the knack of yonks ago.' Martin Holbeach was late for breakfast, too. He sat down in the seat diagonally opposite

Crispin's. 'Mind you, I never eat breakfast normally. I suppose you haven't seen my son anywhere, have you – the big one, I mean?'

Crispin had only the vaguest mental picture of a stooping denimed youth. 'No, I don't think so.'

'Somebody's always missing,' remarked Martin gloomily. 'I suppose you don't know where one can buy an English newspaper, do you?'

Crispin shook his head. He sorted through the plate of food he'd got himself: bread, cheese, olives, melon. He bit into a large black olive and nearly decapitated a tooth on the stone.

'They're like holidays, olives,' said Martin Holbeach suddenly, watching. 'They seem okay on the outside, but when you get to know them, they're something else again.'

Crispin stared at him with a flicker of interest above his dental pain. 'You don't like holidays, then?'

'Can't abide them. I'm a workaholic. So my wife says. I hate being forced to enjoy myself.'

'I know what you mean,' echoed Crispin.

'Especially with Josh, now.'

'Josh?'

'My eldest. He's seventeen. Completely out of control.'

'Really? I mean, I'm sure he can't be. Can he?'

'He can. Out till all hours. Hardly speaks to us. Goes to school only when he's got nothing better to do. Drugs, sex, drink, you name it, old Josh is the expert. They should be paying him to give them personal and social education at school or whatever they call it these days, not the other way around.'

'So why did he come on holiday with you, then?' Crispin was becoming slightly curious.

'Oh, Josh knows what side of his bread the butter's on, all right. He follows the money. The faint prospect of good times in foreign climes when no one's watching.' Martin paused and chewed, thinking of all the wonderful things his son might at this very moment be up to.

'Some of it's pretty comprehensible, of course,' he went on. 'The young of today have a hard time. It's the fundamental alienation of capitalism. Their labour's not meaningful any more. If it ever was. Got a job, have you? You must have, to bring the wife and kiddies on their hols even to a hole like this.'

'Yes,' admitted Crispin lamely. 'I run a design company.'

'Good for you. I edit a paper called *Socialism Now*. Have you heard of it? Don't worry. I wouldn't expect the MD of a design company to be au fait with the left-wing press. What do you read, yourself? The *Guardian*? The *Independent*? Don't tell me. It's the *Independent*, isn't it? The *Guardian*'s nothing but a down-market rag these days. What was I saying? Oh yes, old Josh . . . Now old Josh, what's the future for him when he leaves school? Supposing he were still at it, I mean?'

Crispin considered.

'It's no joke. Even kids with double firsts from Oxbridge can't find anything to get their teeth into these days.'

This phrase troubled Crispin, who was still dealing with bits of olive stone.

'Mind you, he's had his fair share of problems. Father a Marxist with a private income, mother a shrink. Oh, it's not much of a private income, my old man was in the cement business when people wanted to create rather more solid things than they do now. But it is a contradiction in terms, isn't it? Marxism and money, I mean. We've got a house in France near Beynac, that place with a narrow road by the Dordogne that always gets jammed up in summer, but it takes about 140 hours to drive there and some German tycoon's built a helicopter pad next to it. The other house is in Wales. The Welsh nationalists put a petrol bomb through the letter box two years ago. Gave the sheep a helluva fright. Sandy's a psychotherapist,' continued Martin, while Crispin sought for the right connection, 'but like most of them she's better at other people's interpersonal dynamics than her own. And then there are the sibling problems. Our other two are adopted, you see. Primrose, she's from Pakistan, she's eight years younger than Josh, and Freddie, we picked him up in a Romanian orphanage, he's eleven years younger. Terrible malnutrition, you know; we were running a story on it at the time, before any of the nationals. We gave them local names, to help their ethnic identities along. It's Frederic without the "k". We called Primrose Parminder originally, but she suddenly told us one day to call her Primrose. I blame that chap Bellamy – you know, wildflower programmes on television. Anyway, they're hardly companions for Josh, either of them. Sandy's very occupied by the younger children. She says it's just as well, given Josh's behaviour, but myself, I do wonder sometimes if it isn't the other way around.'

'Yes,' observed Crispin.

'You've got two girls, haven't you? I saw old Josh eyeing them. Good lookers, aren't they? I know I shouldn't say this, but I should watch out for old Josh, if I were you. With the girls, I mean. He's got a prick like a dog's nose.'

Like most of what Martin Holbeach had said, Crispin didn't know how to take this. Should fathers talk about their sons in such irreverential terms? What kind of chap *was* Martin Holbeach? He looked ordinary enough. Like old Josh (or, rather, the other way around), he stooped, his shoulders bent as though over his newspaper in a permanent question mark. The hair on top of his head was missing. His skin was white – not for him the full glare of the Turkish sun; instead he lurked on the patio in a small white linen hat reading Edward Said's *Orientalism*. 'Good book, this,' he would say to Crispin later. 'It's all in the mind, you know. The discourse of Orientalism – though I'm not sure I go along with Said's enthusiasm for Foucault – is the way we in the West *see* the Orient. We treat it as a cipher. It's only another form of colonialism.'

Although Crispin escaped from Martin Holbeach, Dodo's pinger soon sent him to wake his daughters. Their room smelt of stale deodorant and melted chocolate. Piles of clothes lay on the floor round the beds, mixed with tapes and a large quantity of plastic and glass cosmetic bottles. Crispin shouted at them and prodded them both. They rumbled and stirred. Star opened one eye. 'Go away, Dad, it's a holiday. We want to sleep.'

'Your mother says you've got to get up.'

'Tell her to fuck off!' Jade turned over.

'Jade, really!'

'Get us a cup of tea, Dad,' demanded Star sleepily.

'We're not getting up,' confirmed Jade.

'This is Turkey,' pointed out Crispin apropos of the tea.

'Kizi does tea.'

'Who?'

'The waiter.'

'Oh, all right then.'

'He spoils them,' grumbled Dodo to Lisa Upton, as Crispin made his way back from the bar with a tray of tea. 'They can twist him round their little finger. Fingers.' She sighed. 'I wish he could show them some discipline.'

Lisa looked at her curiously. 'Don't you do that?'

'It doesn't work.' Dodo sighed again. Weak mothers, thought Lisa to herself, proud of her own strength. Wimpy Hampstead types who bring up their children afraid of the need to lay down firm boundaries. No wonder there was so much in the media these days about evil children. Children are innocent. It's the parents who have everything to answer for. She felt that particularly strongly when she saw the little angels being delivered for the first time each year to the reception class of the school in which she worked as a domestic helper. Most of their mothers couldn't wait to get rid of them. The children couldn't wipe their own bottoms, let alone tie their shoelaces or remember their own telephone numbers or begin to tell the difference between right and wrong.

Lisa looked admiringly at her daughter, Kelly, in the pool. Kelly was wearing a black one-piece and her snorkelling gear, and was weaving her way in and out of other people's legs like a slimy lizard.

'She's a very good swimmer,' observed Dodo.

'She's good at everything, Kelly. That's the problem. Doesn't know what's good for her.' Dodo tried to work this out. 'Her school says she's very clever, that's why she can't concentrate on anything properly.'

Crispin plonked himself back down again in his chair.

'Well done, darling, was it hard?'

The women laughed. Crispin reached for his walkman and Simon and Garfunkel were soon singing 'The Sound of Silence' soothingly into his ears.

'My Kelly's always up with the lark,' confided Lisa. 'She was like that as a baby. I wish I could get away with as little sleep as that! I always say to Derrick, if I don't get my eight hours, it shows in my face. Thank God for the face doctors is what I say!' She laughed thinly and lit a cigarette, blowing the smoke in Dodo's face. Dodo coughed. 'Oh, sorry. I'm afraid I smoke like a chimney. It's bad for the lungs, but good for the waistline.' She looked down at her own approvingly. 'Oh, you can't see a thing. I had my chin done first. That was a couple of thousand. Then my eyes: fifteen hundred. I'm thinking of having my neck done next. I read an article in *Woman* about it when I was having highlights put in one day – Derrick likes me to look nice. There was this whole family who went in for it. In Newcastle. You know, mother, father, daughter and two sons, I think it was. My Derrick's said no so far, though I think his nose could be improved. But he says it's either that or a new runaround for me. Have you seen those four-wheel-drive Fiat Pandas? I rather fancy one of them. They do a nice sky blue. Would you like some of my sun lotion? It's hypo-allergenic. I've got a delicate skin, and Derrick gets it cheap for me.'

Dodo lifted her fingers to her own face and felt its curves and lines. It was a full, round face: like a moon, she thought. Her finger found the crater of the chicken-pox scar above her left ear – she'd had it very badly when she was sixteen, just before she and Crispin got together. Thank God, she'd never been very vain. A pleasant, ordinarily nice face was what she'd got and it was good enough for her. She didn't bother much with make-up, and she wore her hair in a totally unhighlighted Cleopatra bob.

Jade dived into the pool, followed by Star, who slid in from the steps. The three girls swam in circles round each other, calling out the occasional word, smiling, gesturing. 'Star's too thin,' said Dodo abruptly, 'don't you think?'

'Thin's healthy,' said Lisa, 'you don't want to worry about

it. I'm a size eight still, same as I was as a girl in Pinner.' She stubbed out her cigarette and pulled a bottle of nail varnish and two small purple sponges out of her River Island holdall. 'Toe dividers,' she explained. 'Useful, aren't they?'

'She's very fussy about her food. Won't eat meat, won't eat fruit, won't eat anything cooked and green. It's dreadful.'

Lisa nodded. 'It's hard not to worry, isn't it, when there's all that stuff on telly and in the papers about anorexia and bul—
. . . bul— what's it called?'

'Bulimia.'

'That's it. Did you see that awful programme a few weeks ago about the young girl who died? Her mother looked after her. I wonder how it starts,' reflected Lisa, sticking the purple sponges in between her toes and unscrewing the nail polish, which was a virulent magenta colour. 'They say it's to do with the relationship with the mother, don't they? I'm lucky. My Kelly eats like a horse.'

Dodo thinks back to when Star was little. What did she do wrong?

'What colour is their hair really?' asked Lisa critically, the nail polish brush poised over her big toe.

'Star's is blonde like her father. Jade's is brown like mine. They're threatening to have nose rings next.'

'Are you going to let them?'

'How can I stop them? It could be worse. They've already got four holes in one ear, and three in the other. I took them to a chemist the first time. You can't be too careful these days, with AIDS and all that, can you? Then they went off and had the others done at a shady sauna parlour in the Kentish Town Road.'

'I wouldn't worry about it,' said Lisa, congratulating herself again. Her Kelly was sharp, but she didn't really give her a lot of trouble that she noticed. 'They say boys are worse.'

'Are they?'

Lisa considered. 'They say it's their hormones. And then there's the worry about homosexuality. They say that's in the brain now, don't they? I think all this talk about it gives them the wrong idea. It encourages them. Gay! What kind of word is that? Most of them are miserable sods, always complaining about everything.' She wrinkled her nose as though objecting to an unpleasant smell in the air.

Lying on his sunbed insufficiently protected by factor twenty, but with Simon and Garfunkel melodiously guarding him from having to listen to the women's conversation, Crispin was thinking again about Meg of the golden bikini. That first image of her poised on the edge of the circle of blue backlit by the sun and wrapped in two ribbons of gold kept representing itself to him, as though trying to make a point of some kind.

But what kind of point? What did this figure of Meg, poised between water, earth and sky, symbolize? Freedom? Flight? Crispin rejected the most obvious answer to his question – that he fancied her. For all his faults (and there were many of these), he had always been faithful to Dodo. Mostly it'd been from disinclination to organize anything else. Now, after nearly thirty years, he wondered if it might be fear. But whatever it was, it added up to the same result: Dodo had never had any cause to doubt his bodily fidelity to her.

Disney Stafford always teased Crispin about his lack of knowledge of women (a huge lack compared to Disney's own), but Crispin himself was much more troubled by other features of the passing of the years, and particularly lately by a gnawing feeling of disenchantment that he seemed to carry round with him all the time, like an olive stone wedged against the nerve of a tooth. In the dream he'd had yesterday, it had come back to him: sitting in the senior study of the Hatfield School on a June evening, with the red-tendrilled honeysuckle framing the moonlit sky and the garden with its ordered fragrances, he had been possessed of a hopefulness about life, by a sense of meaning and of mission, that had been quite as heady as the night air. He had been looking forward to everything – to tomorrow and the day after that, and to the next year, to the new people he would meet and the new things he would do, to the feelings and thoughts he would have and the way all of this would be intertwined like the honeysuckle and the door frame to provide a sense of flow between oneself and life-out-there, between what is and what is perceived to be. The fact that Crispin had never, as his father repetitively said, done much with his life, was neither here nor there. It wasn't about doing things – it was about wanting to be alive, rather than merely living by default, because you couldn't think of anything better to do.

Crispin uncovered an eye and looked at the sun. The same sun as shone and set on those days of his boyhood and extended youth. Peace, love, happiness! He and Dodo had lain in lush daisied fields with loud music – Pink Floyd, the Beatles – in their ears, just *being*. That was it, there was no time for just *being* now. In order just to be, one must lack a sense of time – there must be all the time in the world.

Crispin was so impressed by his definition of the problem that he put out a hand to make connection with Dodo on the adjacent sunbed, so that he could tell her. But the sunbed was empty. Lisa Upton, seeing Crispin's gesture, said, 'She's just gone in for a minute. She said she was going to find out about a trip to the mud baths.'

In those flower-filled days, Crispin had thought Dodo was quite the most wonderful woman: generous without turning it into an art, capable without making you feel guilty; warm, cherishing, funny. He couldn't – can't – imagine life without her. Particularly now, when life had become such a mundane struggle. Up at seven thirty every day, to the office by eight thirty, meetings all day, a sandwich at one's desk for lunch, home at seven. Hearing about Dodo's day and greeting the ill-mannered Jade and her less ill-mannered sister; juggling the evenings: who was eating what with whom and what time they were to be in by. A snatched drink or two in the study/ironing room at the top of the house, looking out across the moneyed rooftops to the lit ice-cream block of the Royal Free Hospital and, in the other direction, the grassy hats of Hampstead Heath. It wasn't as though there was anything *wrong* with any of it. It was just that one was running hard all the time in order to continue to stand in exactly the same spot.

Time again. All the time. No time. What's the time? Who cares?

'Crispin! You're asleep again!'

'I'm not,' he protested.

Something wet landed on his legs. Star's flippers. 'Look after these for me, Dad. I'm just going into town with Jade and Kelly.'

'No, you're not,' said Dodo, 'it's lunchtime.'

'We'll have it there.'

'What do you think, Crispin?'

'Oh, all right then.'

'Thanks, Dad.'

Dodo gave him a filthy look, but he didn't see it because he was looking the other way. Divested of their offspring, he and Dodo ate lunch alone. They had a bottle of wine to celebrate. Crispin ordered octopus salad, which was a disappointing mélange of portions of Star's flippers mixed with beans, the whole coated in a thick, sweet mayonnaise. Crispin told Dodo his revelation about time. Dodo was worried about him. What did he mean? What was he doing, thinking about such deep things on holiday?

She changed the subject. She and Lisa Upton had organized a collective trip to the mud baths. 'It's a hundred and four thousand lire for the boat,' she explained. 'That's only ten thousand four hundred each between the ten of us. Isn't that amazing? It'll be fun to go with the Uptons, don't you think? Jade and Star seem to be getting on so well with Kelly.'

'I'm not sure about Kelly,' he remarked, though more from intuition than on the basis of any real evidence.

The boat was painted blue and white like most of those in Karput and was called *Tinfan 2*. 'I wonder what happened to *Tinfan 1*?' joked Derrick Upton, but Crispin, who'd never felt safe in any kind of boat, didn't find this funny. He sat unsurely with his feet on the sun-faded cotton carpet in the middle of one side, feeling that he'd been pressured into doing something he never really chose – again. The three girls had commandeered the prow. They were busy swapping tapes to put in their Walkmans; Dire Straits, REM, the Levellers.

Wilma Blake, Derrick Upton's mother, had come on the trip, too. She sat opposite Crispin, her feet squarely on the floor of the boat. She was about five feet two, had white hair, and resembled a cross between a character out of *The Little House on the Prairie* and one from *The Golden Girls* – that is, until you heard her speak, when her Midlands accent gave the game away. She wore black lace-up shoes and thick tights for her varicose veins. She gripped her black handbag with both hands on her lap as though it were some sort of defence against untoward happenings.

Kizi Demir gave them a hand cutting loose from the mooring by the hotel pool and bar. It was always interesting to see who got on with whom on these holidays. Some people were loners. Some families appeared desperate to reach out for others to share the strain of being on holiday with. Mehmet Lorca, the manager, ran the hotel deliberately to encourage these sorts of groups – the restaurant tables and the boats were all team-size.

The Delanceys and the Uptons and Wilma Blake moved off up the river, past the harbours and the riverside cafés and post-card, t-shirt and trinket stalls. Soon they were away from the town and in the middle of the wide amber river. A rockface cut them off from the sun for a while, and then the river swung round and they were treated to a shining stream of gold. 'How far is it, Mum?' asked Stevie Upton.

'Only about twenty minutes, sweetheart.'

'That's enough for me, I'm sure,' said Mrs Blake. She smiled at Crispin. 'And for you, too, Mr Delancey?'

'I'm okay,' said Crispin defensively.

They moored alongside a dozen or so other boats. 'He'll wait for us,' Derrick explained in a tour-leader fashion, 'however long we are. That's the system here. So we can take our time.'

The walk up a hill and through a field to the mud baths took Crispin back to the school science laboratory. The smell of sulphur was overpowering. The children were delighted by it – even the sophisticated Jade unplugged her earphones, as though unblocking the ears was necessary to allow the smell in properly. There was a board which said in five different languages that covering oneself in mud removed ten years. 'That means if we do it twice, we won't be born yet!' observed Jade and Star correctly.

'Well, that would solve a few problems, wouldn't it,' muttered Crispin uncharacteristically to himself.

It really was a disgusting sight: a small flat area, about ten metres by forty, set between rocky crags on what appeared to be an uninhabited island, surfaced with grey-brown gelatinous mud. On the left, two pools were sunk into the mud, each about five feet deep. The pools had rails around, and steps going down, and there were more multi-lingual signs. On the right, there was a clear river stream – at least it would have been clear had there not been such a demand for its services. There was one cold shower, but the queue for it was Russian in size. There were about a hundred and fifty people there, all of them either trying to make the mud stick to their skins or trying equally hard to get it off. As might be imagined, their efforts were accompanied by much shrieking and laughter, and many exclamations of disgust.

'Well I never!' said Wilma Blake. 'What can they all be thinking of? I think I'll just sit here and have a glass of water.'

There was a small café selling mud-free drinks and pastries next to the shower.

'Come on,' said Kelly to Jade and Star, 'let's go for it.'

'What about you, darling?' inquired Dodo.

'I don't think so,' admitted Crispin.

'Go on, Daddy! If you don't, I won't, either!'

Kelly and Jade gave Star a withering look and strode off into the mud.

'Here you are, Mother,' said Lisa Upton, passing over her capacious holdall, 'you can look after our things.'

'Rather you than me, dear,' said the old lady cheerfully. 'I should take that chain off, Derrick. And what about your engagement ring, Lisa? And your cross? Would you like me to look after it for you, dearie?'

Derrick Upton unzipped his video camera.

'Where's Simon?'

'Has anyone seen Simon?'

'He'll turn up,' said Mrs Blake comfortably. 'You go off and enjoy yourselves. And mind the mud on that machine of yours!'

In the furthest pool Kelly and Jade were already practising. The trick was to yank up handfuls of the stuff from the bottom of the pool and squeeze the moisture out of it before applying it to the skin. There was an art to this, as there was to everything. A couple of local young men showed Kelly and Jade how to do it. Since the girls weren't very good, the young men offered them some of their own mud. One of them had a huge bank of the stuff on a rock ledge above the pool. He handed a dollop of it to the girls: 'Please!'

'I never would have thought I'd be grateful for someone giving me a load of mud,' observed Jade. 'What do we do about our hair, do you think?'

Her purple tresses were already streaked with mud. One of the young men indicated that she was supposed to tie it up. 'Where you stay?' he asked.

'At the Hotel Rhapsody Palas.'

'Ah.'

Kelly giggled. 'At least he saw you without the mud first.' She herself was mud-enclosed from head to waist and was now getting out of the pool to deal with the rest of her body. With her cropped hair and thin boyish figure, she looked like a Victorian chimney sweep. Jade saw her mother approaching in her broad red swimsuit. Dodo was closely followed by Lisa Upton, and the two women started throwing mud at each other while Derrick Upton zoomed in on them with his camera. 'Don't you sometimes wish they'd just go away?' sighed Kelly, watching Jade watching them.

Under the trees away from the mud, but not its smell, Crispin and Star Delancey and Wilma Blake sat drinking Turkish mineral water and looking after everybody's clothes. Out of the corner of his eye, Crispin saw something moving by one of the fences, next to the men's changing room. It looked like a pair of binoculars. He leant forward to see better, but the person behind the binoculars wore a hat and dark glasses and could be any variety of watcher of birds or other species.

'There's someone outside looking in,' he said.

'There usually is.' Wilma Blake nodded knowingly.

Crispin shook his own head to clear it. 'Do you like it in Turkey, Mrs Blake?' he asked, to change the subject.

'Goodness gracious, no, I only came to please Derrick!' She gave a minor witch-like laugh. 'I can't abide towns, for a start. I live in a little village called Diddington about twenty miles outside Leicester. Number 5 Cutting Lane. I was born there. I buried both my husbands from there – Derrick's father and then Mr Blake – one had a bad heart and the other bad lungs. If I could have taken the best of both of them I would have got a good 'un, wouldn't I?'

She chortled. Crispin wondered how old she was. Seventy? Seventy-five? Eighty? He leant forward across the table to take a closer look at her. Her skin was yellowish, swarthy almost. It was the same colour all over. Her eyes were coal black behind black-rimmed glasses and her eyebrows were dark as well. Topped with the cloud of whitish grey hair, the whole gave an appearance of ferocity concentrated around the eyes, although she had a mole on her chin with a couple of hairs growing out of it.

Wilma Blake took a white cotton handkerchief out of her handbag and mopped her brow.

'Would you like me to get you another drink?'

'I'd better not, thank you, or I'll be wanting to spend a penny, and I shouldn't like to have to do that here.'

It was still very hot. Crispin tugged at his t-shirt. 'You know those turtles, Dad,' said Star suddenly. 'Kizi says there are boats going to the beach where they are after dark. It's illegal, though.' It was easy to imagine the baby turtles striking out on some fatally erroneous journey towards a tourist torch. Star was the environmentally minded Delancey. She hadn't eaten meat since she was six. At ten she'd asked for a subscription to Greenpeace for her birthday, and the next year it was half a penguin in London Zoo. They used to go and look at him, poor Joey, locked in the penguin house with forty others.

Poor Star, like Joey living in the shadow of others – in this case her elder sister by ten months, Jade Elizabeth. They'd given both girls conventional middle names to make up for unusual first ones – Star was Star Victoria. Dodo and he had originally banned children from their horizons – the world, in the days of CND and the Committee of 100, seemed far too unsound for one to inflict it on the unborn. Then Dodo got older (and so did he, but it didn't seem to affect him in the same way), and there was the usual stuff about the pill and high blood pressure, and then some mucking around with a rubber device that resembled a soap dish, and then Dodo was pregnant and they didn't get round to doing anything about an abortion, and then there was Jade. She was born with thick hair and the usual rosy infant limbs and sharp blue-green eyes with huge silky lashes. Crispin hadn't been able to get over her beauty. Every bit of Jade the baby had been pure, untouched perfection. From then on it had all been downhill, especially now, he reflected, watching one mud-covered Barbie dancing hand in hand with another by a sulphur pool with every male in the vicinity watching. And then, hardly had they got used to Jade when Star arrived. Dodo had tried breastfeeding them both, but it was hopeless, so she put them both on the bottle. Crispin used to take Star into his office and shut the door, while Dodo dealt with Jade. There was nothing but him and the baby and a bottle and a spare nappy. He would feed her and change her and rock her to sleep. As a consequence, he'd always felt a special bond with her, though what she felt was a mystery to him.

'Where are you going?' Crispin asked accusingly as Star got up from the table.

'To look for Simon.'

'That's right,' said the old lady approvingly. 'He's probably gone on one of his "recces" as he calls them. He likes to know where he is, does our Simon.'

'Don't we all,' added Crispin sadly.

'Yes, Mr Delancey. And don't you think I sometimes wonder where I am? Derrick feels guilty about me. I live on my own, he thinks that's a state to pity, but it isn't. Lisa doesn't want me, I'm an old bore to her. I don't blame her, I felt the same about my own mother-in-law. I only had one of those,' she explained, 'Mr Blake's parents had passed on by the time I came on the scene. Their home was struck by lightning.'

'I'm sorry to hear that,' said Crispin.

'So were they, I expect.' She laughed her witch-like laugh again. It was a surprisingly deep noise, coming from somewhere fundamental inside her, like the sulphur and the mud pools. 'I said why don't we go to Devon or Wales or somewhere nice like that. But no, Lisa wanted the sun. Myself, I would have been happy to stay in Cutting Lane. I like this time of year; harvest time. The combines are out till late, I find their clug-clugging a great comfort. The rose by my cottage door, "Compassion", always flowers for a second time about now. Have you ever seen a harvest moon, Mr Delancey?' Crispin shook his head; Mrs Blake was going to describe one anyway. 'It's a great blood red thing stuck like an orange in the navy blue of the summer sky. It's very low, so low you think it's going to hit the fields and explode like some sort of bomb. I sit in my bedroom window and look out across the top of the elder tree and I just watch it, night after night. I'd rather watch that than any television show.'

Crispin listened to Wilma Blake and tried to imagine the harvest moon in Cutting Lane. But it was just too hot and sulphurous here – there was far too much reality for the imagination to work. She reminded him of Mrs Moore in Forster's *A Passage to India*. But there was something odd about Wilma Blake. He couldn't put his finger on it. Her speech about the country had been almost too practised, too pat. But then perhaps she'd given it too many times. He pushed the feeling of oddity away.

They left the mud island just before six o'clock. Star located Simon down by the harbour trying to make it off to the South Seas in an empty boat, and Jade and Kelly shook off their young men with a series of vague 'we'll sees'. Derrick had forgotten to take his chain off, and the sulphur in the mud had turned it an odd greenish colour. He video-d them leaving the site, but Crispin had to go back because he'd forgotten his sunglasses. As he climbed up the last bit of the hill and reached the short signposted path to the mud pools he saw what was either an illusion or reality: Meg Shaw, her golden bikini and golden self entirely mud-caked and shining with silvery late afternoon light.

THREE

Sweet Sixteen

Meg Shaw was reading *Dracula*. The book had been recommended by her colleague Gail Gillespie, an educational social
worker whose own vampire-like imagination gave her a real
insight into the problems of children and young people.

Meg sat by the pool with the book propped against her
knees. Across the pool, two of the bird-watching women lay
sunning themselves. They were both called Joan. One had
recently been widowed, and the other was her friend. There
had been two spare bird-watching places at Rhapsody Palas, so
they'd come along at the suggestion of Gareth Barrett, the
founder of the Cardiff branch of the European Bird-watching
Society. Today Barrett and the others were off in literally hot
pursuit of the (male) lemon-breasted black-headed bunting, a
bird renowned for its reverse migratory habits. The two Joans
had stayed behind, as they were feeling a bit tired as a result of
yesterday's scramble after the same in the hills above Moybat
beach. They smiled pleasantly at Meg, their white flesh oozing
out of their Lycra swimsuits, and their toenails, painted a
carmine red, glinting garishly in the sun.

There was a lot of red stuff in *Dracula*. Blood, the life-force,
is what women give but also remove. Femininity and female
sexuality are at odds; strange currents undercut the pale polite
faces of Mina Harker and the unfortunate Lucy Westenra. Meg

was lost in the Victorian dialogues. Aaron passed her chair, guidebook in hand. 'I'm going to look at the rock tombs. I'll be back by four.'

'Okay.' She lifted her eyes from the page. 'Have you got some money? What about lunch?'

'Yes, and don't worry, I've got some stuff from breakfast and a bottle of water.'

She knew he would have. Aaron was very self-reliant, very well organized. When they went out together at home it was always Aaron who remembered the front door key.

On his way to cross the river, Aaron met Martin Holbeach, prowling restlessly round the hotel grounds. The river crossings were accomplished either by a boy who couldn't have been more than ten or so, or by a grandmother with black eyes nestled like currants in a brown beaten bun of a face. Aaron got in the old woman's boat. There was a slight wind this morning. It lifted the corners of the blue and white scarf she had tied round her hair. Martin watched while she rowed Aaron across. He thought nostalgically about the *Socialism Now* office – about its chaotic bustle, strong black coffee, circular debates, and the perpetual motion of its fax machine. He knew what was going to happen now – Sandy was going to ask him to take Primrose and Freddie off her hands for a bit. He felt sorry for the kids, but he didn't really feel they were his. They belonged to Sandy, if they belonged to anyone.

He decided to avoid Sandy by walking round the back of the hotel into reception, instead of through the gardens and by the pool. By the reception desk, he met Crispin, flushed with sun. Martin looked at him critically, which was the usual way he looked at anyone.

'I've overdone it a bit,' admitted Crispin pinkly. 'It happens every year. I thought I'd see if there were any excursions I could go on, you know, away from the sun.' He waved a printed timetable. 'The problem is, they all seem to have left for today.'

'There are the Turkish baths in Ocakkoy,' said Mehmet Lorca, the Rhapsody Palas's manager, helpfully. He was quite used to restless sunburnt Englishmen.

'Too hot,' complained Crispin.

'We do have bicycles for hire,' tried Mehmet again. 'They are good Raleigh mountain bicycles. We have them serviced every year. Eight thousand lire hire per day.'

'Dodo's always telling me I need some exercise,' observed Crispin.

'Wives are all the same, aren't they?' commented Martin sexistly. 'Why don't we, then?'

'I can just put it on the bill, if you like,' offered Mehmet.

'Well . . .' said Crispin indecisively.

'Come on, old chap, it'll do us both good. I'll pay, it won't break the bank.'

They set off with a badly drawn map of the area. Crispin plastered himself with factor twenty. 'I'll have to keep to the shady side of the road.'

'You do that.'

Crispin took the map and held it one way and then the other. 'I'm not very good at direction.'

Martin pointed: 'The lake's that way. There must be a road round it. Why don't we aim for Kracjek at the northern end? We could get a drink and something to eat there.'

'Sounds good.'

Crispin's saddle began to hurt almost immediately. He stopped. 'I think it's at a funny angle.' He found a spanner in

42

the bag and adjusted it. 'That's better.' The road was downhill at first. He watched Martin cycling ahead of him. The bicycle, a bright pink, was too small for him. His white legs stuck out sideways like underbaked French croissants.

You couldn't really call it a road – it was more like a line of craters strung together with islands of stone. The trick was to keep your eyes down so you avoided falling into them. It was worse when the craters went uphill, and especially when the relative positions of the sun and the tall rocks on their left stripped the road of shade. Sweat dripped into Crispin's eyes, and he was about to suggest they stop, when he noticed that Martin had already done so. He dropped his bicycle into the scrub at the side of the road and looked down. Beneath him, the lake was a motionless gaudy blue. It went on and on into the distance, edged with olives and other greenery, and with bleached white stones.

'Magnificent, isn't it?' said Martin.

Crispin nodded wetly.

Martin took his shirt off. Crispin looked at him. 'Here – you'd better have some of my factor twenty.' He dug around in the saddle bag parked among the spiky bushes. Pine and eucalyptus combined with the chemical odours of the suntan lotion in an odd aroma.

'Can you do my back?' Martin handed Crispin the bottle. Crispin took it and paused for a moment before starting to rub the cream over Martin's white back. It was curiously flawless – no spots, moles or scars – and soft, as though it had never heard the word muscle. It was like a baby's skin. 'Further down as well,' instructed Martin, 'we're going to have the sun on our backs all the way from now on.' Crispin dabbed the white cream on the knobs in Martin's spine and spread it sideways just above the waist of his jeans. He felt queasy suddenly.

'That feels good.'

Crispin snapped the lid back on the bottle. It was overwhelmingly hot. In the midday heat, very little moved in the countryside, except for the stridulations of grasshoppers and crickets' wings, and the slithery movements of a couple of Aesculapian snakes climbing a nearby cypress tree. He moved away from Martin and put the bottle back in his saddle bag. 'How far is Kracjek, do you think?'

Martin studied the useless map, and looked from it to the repetitive blue curves of the lake shores below. 'It's hard to tell. I don't think this road is exactly marked on the map. We'll just have to go on until we get there.'

There was hardly any traffic on the road. A couple of cars, and then a tourist bus, honked at them enthusiastically. Martin had tied a handkerchief over his head to protect it. Crispin's legs hurt. He practised pulling in his stomach muscles on the easy bits. 'This must be doing us a lot of good,' he remarked hopefully.

Every now and then, they came to clusters of tumbledown houses, with pale chickens running around, and tethered white goats with thin beards and mournful expressions. The paint on the houses was always peeling, and strips of corrugated iron lay in the place of proper roofs. The washing hung on ropes strung between the houses was old and full of holes. But everywhere the drabness was lit by the golden light of the Mediterranean sun, and by flamboyant red roses, the colour of the two Joans' toenails and of the vampires' blood in the book Meg Shaw was reading by the pool in the Hotel Rhapsody Palas. Through one doorway Crispin and Martin saw women, their bodies and heads covered in thick cotton, beating kapok into shape to stuff pillows for sale in the cheap town shops. 'It's a very poor country, you know,' said Martin on a flat stretch that allowed for conversation. 'Over half the population work on the land, and an awful lot of the poor buggers go to become *Gastarbeiters* in Germany. Suffers from being caught between cultures: Orientalism and Western capitalism. Both bad in different ways. Atatürk may have sorted out the alphabet in seven weeks but he didn't begin to understand the infrastructure.' He gazed reflectively around him. 'You look at the scenery – the lakes and the mountains could be Switzerland or Norway. But then you see the people and the conditions they live in.'

'It's immoral really to be a tourist in a place like this, isn't it?' countered Crispin, struck by the thought that he really shouldn't be here at all.

'Tourists and drugs: what else can Turkey make money out of? But these people,' Martin gestured at the villages either side of the road, taking his hands off the bicycle and swerving wildly, 'how does it help them? They make their living from the land. Just about. Some of the young people may be able to get jobs in the tourist centres but they're badly paid, and it destroys the local cultural fabric. This is still a Moslem country. Families worry about the morals of their girls and the young men can be sucked into some of our nasty Western ways.'

The road round the lake went on and on. Martin took his handkerchief off and scratched his sweaty head. 'I could kill for a beer.'

Crispin stood his bike against a rock and sat down in a minute portion of shade. 'The town must be *somewhere*. Was this wise, I ask myself?' he said.

'You mean you're asking me?'

Crispin closed his eyes and laid his head back against the

warm rock. Martin mopped his head. In the dense hot silence, something bigger moved on the mountainside above, and a couple of golden rocks made their way down, crashing through the dehydrated undergrowth. Both men jumped like startled schoolboys, and then looked up to where a couple of goats peered over the edge, their stringy beards outlined against the thick blue of the sky.

'Bloody hell!' said Crispin.

'Jesus Christ!' said Martin.

'D'you think we should go back, perhaps?' Crispin was beginning to hold the Hotel Rhapsody Palas, and family life at the poolside with Dodo's pinger, in a new, fonder regard.

'Your legs giving you trouble, are they?'

'Aren't yours?'

'I tell you what, old chap, we'll go on for half an hour and if we can't see anything then we'll go back.'

Kracjek appeared in a cove round a cliff twenty minutes later. They dropped down the hill at such a pace that when Crispin braked near the bottom his back brake flew off into a clump of pinks. 'Shit! So much for Mehmet's annual servicing.' He got off and scrabbled around in the stones by the edge of the road looking for it.

'One's enough,' observed Martin, stopping behind him. 'As the bishop said to the actress.' He chortled. 'This is the land of eunuchs anyway – some of them were only half castrated, you know. The white ones, that is. The black ones had both their balls cut off.'

'What's that got to do with it?'

'Nothing, really. Come on, let's find the local tavern, we've earned it.'

Martin seemed to have taken control. He ordered plentifully

at the first café they came to, and plates of meat and vegetables and salad arrived, along with bottles of beer the colour of the roadside sun. 'God, I'm glad Sandy's not here,' he reflected noisily between mouthfuls. 'I can get stuck into some real meat for a change, and I don't have to eat a salad. I *hate* salad, don't you? All that munching, I can't be doing with it myself.'

Crispin began to feel better, that is less hungry and thirsty.

'Where d'you live, Delancey?'

'Hampstead. It's . . .' Crispin began to explain.

'So do we. What road?'

'Tanza.'

'We're in Nassington. We can probably see your back garden from ours. Is your house collapsing into the clay of the under-ground river like ours? Daft place to build. Thank God we haven't got a cellar. You haven't either, have you? We've got some friends down the hill, he's a lawyer which is just as well, their house is flooded in filthy water for six months of the year. You like living in Hampstead, do you?'

'It's all right.'

'You mean you can't think of anywhere you'd rather be? Given that you're stuck with the family and the job and you've got to live somewhere where you can be a good citizen and a good family man and all that?'

Crispin's a bit shocked to hear his own semi-articulated thoughts spoken so baldly.

'I can see that you agree with me. It's hard for us men, isn't it? That's what the feminists don't understand. I hope for your sake your wife isn't one of them. Fortunately, Sandy isn't, though sometimes I think it'd be better for her if she was. Do you *like* your wife, Delancey?'

Crispin opened his mouth to say, of course I do, but Martin

got there first. 'I mean *like* rather than *love*. It's a different thing, you know. I can't stand Sandy myself. Her conversation's boring, and she's frightened of change. For her the future's just the same as the past, only worse, because she doesn't know what's going to happen in it. But I'm fond of her, don't get me wrong. I suppose that's what we men call love. She tries hard. Well, so do I, come to that!' He laughed and tipped the remains of a bottle of beer down his throat. 'Now, how would you like to have that on your grave: "He tried hard".'

Crispin thinks.

'Men and women aren't made for one another, that's my opinion.' Martin put his elbows on the table and his face rather close to Crispin's. 'It's in the nature of a dialectical struggle that never gets anywhere because no material resolution is possible, don't you think?'

'I've never thought about it like that.'

'We've all got both genders in us anyway, whatever sex we are. Interesting distinction that – invented by some female sociologist back in the early seventies. We may be biologically male or biologically female, but there's something seductive about the trappings of the other gender, and I don't mean sexually, either. Of course, that only makes the whole thing even more impossible. Men fight women, but we're really fighting ourselves. Don't you think, Delancey?'

Crispin swallowed hard.

'And what about the kids, Delancey? What about the generation gap? I must say, I don't understand the little buggers. You give them everything and all they want to do is wander around in the same pair of jeans with holes in for a year, smoking and popping pills and blasting their ears with foul music. I must say,' Martin Holbeach seemed to have to say quite a lot, 'the first time I saw one of those personal stereos, I thought the poor devil was disabled and those were special microphones in his ears. I expect they do disable you. Eventually. Our kids'll be deaf by the time they're forty. Do you ever try to talk to yours about how they should look after themselves just in case they get to be the dreadful age we are? Well, first of all you've got to get them to take those things out of their ears, and then you've got to make them listen. The first is easier than the second. Old Josh tells me we adults have made a fucking mess of everything and he doesn't fucking care. Their language is another thing. It's hardly musical, is it?'

'You're right,' said Crispin at last. 'It's as though they're another species. But I'm sure they say the same about us.'

'Tell me about your work, Delancey, and I'll shut up for a bit.'

At four o'clock, they were still there, and as the waiter had been replenishing their supply of beer without being asked to, they'd got through quite a lot.

'We're never going to make it back to Karput, you know,' observed Crispin philosophically. 'Especially not without my back brake.'

'We'll get a boat, then, that's what we'll do.'

It cost quite a bit, relatively speaking, to find a boat that would take them and the bicycles across the lake back to Karput. The owner had a large stereo fixed in the middle which was playing the theme from *Out of Africa*. It was cold in the boat and it got colder as they advanced towards the centre of the lake. Crispin shivered, and crossed his arms. 'You can cuddle up to me, if you like,' offered Martin. 'I never feel the cold. It's just as well. Sandy's like an iceberg – it's one of our few compatibilities. Mind you,' he trailed his hand in the clear icy water outside the boat, 'these hot flushes she gets these days are warming her up a bit. Is your wife into hot flushes and so forth, Delancey?'

Crispin supposed not, as he hadn't heard about them. He decided to go on feeling cold rather than snuggle up to Martin. In fact, he pretended not to feel cold any more. Halfway across the lake Martin announced his bladder wouldn't make it, and he stood up and urinated what looked like unprocessed beer on to the back of a passing turtle.

'Where *have* you been?' said the wives in unison when they returned the bicycles to Mehmet in the hotel reception. Dodo and Sandy had been interrogating Mehmet about what he'd done with their husbands. 'You mean you hired a *whole* boat to come back?' Dodo was probably flushed with anger under her suntan.

'As opposed to half a one?' muttered Martin. 'Don't worry, Mrs D., I paid anyway.'

'You didn't even have cycling helmets,' complained Sandy. 'That's setting a very bad example for the children.'

'I don't think they *have* cycling helmets in Karput.'

Crispin decided not to mention the broken back brake.

'We were worried, Dad,' said Star later. 'What did you want to go off like that for without telling us where you were going?'

'Why didn't you ring?' demanded Jade. 'That's what you'd say if it were us. It's double standards, that's what it is!' She sulked off, with Star following. If Joshua had been there, he wouldn't have minced his words either, but he was kissing a young woman from Karput in the office of the local boat co-operative, between the green screen of an illegally imported Amstrad and a pile of printed flags covered in turtles.

'Calm down,' said Crispin to his family. 'You ought to be

pleased that I've taken some exercise. *And* I didn't get sunburnt, *and* you've had a nice peaceful day without me.' He tried to beam paternally. 'I'll take you out to dinner tonight,' he offered, finally.

It was the last thing he felt like, but that undoubtedly wasn't important.

'It's no use arguing,' said Dodo when the girls tried to turn down his invitation, 'we're going to eat out tonight.'

'Why do we always have to do what *you* say? It's only because you're cross with Dad and he's trying to make it up to you. You shouldn't involve us in your petty quarrels.'

Crispin came out of the shower. 'You may have had other plans,' he told his daughters, under the influence of a whole day listening to Martin Holbeach's managerial style, 'but this is a family holiday and you're coming with us.'

Jade's dark eyes were full of bullets. She tossed her long hair defiantly over a tanned shoulder which supported a series of irregularly textured straps: fine white broderie anglaise, rough black cotton in varying widths. 'Is that what you're going to wear, darling?' asked Dodo, trying to be diplomatic.

'You mean why don't I put on a pretty frock and some proper shoes?'

'Don't be rude to your mother, Jade.'

'I haven't got a pretty frock, anyway, and I didn't bring any other shoes. Nor did Star. We've only got our DMs.'

Dodo marched them all out of the hotel like a mother duck. She chose the path by the river towards Karput. It skirted several building sites – the shells of hotels abandoned midway through their construction due to bungled planning permission – and also the houses of boatmen, rough and ready part colour-washed affairs fronted by gaggles of brown-limbed children who watched the Delanceys, in their smart tourist clothes, picking their way carefully through the loose stones of the river path.

Dodo took Crispin's arm; they walked ahead of the girls. 'I didn't really mind you going off today with Martin Holbeach,' she said. 'I only got worried when you were late back. I thought you'd had an accident.' Crispin remembered the goats, and the falling rocks, but they came in the same class as the broken brake, and he said nothing. 'What's he like, Martin? Is he as domineering as he seems?' Crispin thought he probably was, and went on to tell her about the discovery of the proximate Hampstead living circumstances, as he knew this would interest her. 'Isn't it amazing?' enthused Dodo. 'You have to come to Turkey to meet your next-door neighbours!' She would have gone on to use the phrase 'small world', had Jade not kicked a rock viciously towards them. 'Jade's only doing it to get at me,' said Dodo. 'If anybody else wants to take on organizing you lot, that's fine by me. Do you think I enjoy it? It's certainly not my idea of a holiday.'

Crispin could feel Dodo's indignation bursting out of her along with the warm perspiration of her bare half-bronzed arm pressed against the clean blue shirt she had invited (told) him to put on. He had thought that dinner out was his idea, but like most such, he left its organization to other people. He wondered, if it wasn't Dodo's idea of a holiday and it wasn't his, why had they come on it? He glanced back at the girls; Jade was in front of Star, her arms folded, her steamy unlaced DMs kicking the stones. She looked like a thunderstorm. Behind her, Star tried to appear casually uninvolved. She was picking at a knot in her hair.

'It's only another couple of years,' he said to reassure their mother. 'Then they'll be off, and we can do what we like.'

He didn't believe it, and he didn't want it. As a matter of fact, as he uttered these words he felt suddenly and surprisingly quite sick at the prospect of life without Jade and Star – at the prospect of the same thing day after day, the same tedious struggles at Delancey Designs, the same effort to find a place to park the car in Tanza Road, round the corner from Martin Holbeach's own similar struggles in Nassington Road, but without these vibrant youngsters, these intimations of immortality, waiting to bait him at every turn. Rather abruptly, he detached Dodo's warm arm from his. 'Sorry,' he said, 'it's a bit hot.'

She took a pace sideways, like a crab, to make a point. 'I can see I'm not popular tonight.'

'Sorry,' he mumbled again. 'I'm probably overtired, because of the cycle ride.'

They came into the centre of Karput. Pale trees perspired in front of the minaret. To the left was a large green sculpture of a turtle, and a little further over one of a small brass man kicking a football. Both the turtle and the footballer had been planted round by marigolds. Their bright button heads were the colour of the strips of gold trailed by the setting sun across the sky. A sign to the Delanceys' right said 'Special Turkish Food', and a painted board listed various delicacies, including 'omlit', 'bonfrit', 'grilled mead boll', 'lamp spit', and 'spagety bolonez'.

'Shall we go in here?' suggested Crispin, hungrily.

'Lisa Upton told me where we ought to go – it was recommended by the girl from Proper Holidays,' fired Dodo from barely opened lips. She led them down a side street to a place with tables on a mud floor and coloured lights on the trees and a sign strung across the entrance saying 'Dircan Family Restaurant'. Dodo pointed to some illuminated cases of food by the door: 'We have to go over there and choose what we want to eat.'

Jade said, 'I'm not coming, I only want chips.'

Star said, 'I'll just have some bread.'

Dodo gave her a penetrative look. 'You need a good square meal.'

'Leave me alone, Mum, I'm not hungry.'

Crispin and Dodo went over and inspected the displays. 'Have you noticed how little she's eating these days?' said Dodo. 'You don't think she's anorexic, do you?'

'What?' Crispin was looking closely at the glass case full of food. There was salad – aubergine salad – cold and hot; mushroom salad; cucumber salad; vegetable-stuffed aubergines; stuffed peppers; stews – potato stew, bean stew and lamb stew; and then there was fish – either the backboned or rubbery variety, depending on your mood. Crispin chose red mullet. Dodo said she would have lamb stew. 'No, I don't think so,' he said, in answer to her question, less because he did than because that was what she wanted him to say.

'Well, now,' he said, sitting down again and determined to be cheerful, but finding it difficult to balance his chair on the uneven earth beneath at the same time, 'well, now, tell me, have the mud baths had their effect? Was it worth getting decked up in all that goo?'

Jade glowered. Dodo fiddled with her sandal under the tablecloth.

He tried again. 'What do we think of the holiday so far?' This was even more of a mistake.

'Can we have some water, Dad?' asked Star. 'I'm thirsty.'

He ordered some, and a bottle of wine. As soon as the waitress brought the wine, he filled his and Dodo's glasses, offered the girls some, and then drank his own rather quickly. 'That's better.' He felt the alcohol breaking down the tension in his body, adding to the sedative effects of the beer put there earlier. 'Have a drink,' he said to Dodo. 'It's not bad, this wine.' He started examining the label on the bottle, idly picking at the edges.

'Don't do that!' hissed Dodo. 'I hate it when you do that!'

When Jade had eaten her chips, she got up from the table. 'Thank you for the food,' she said very politely, and not meaning it. 'I think you two should sort out your relationship.' She meant this, but what it meant Crispin wasn't sure. 'We'll meet you back at the hotel later. You coming, Star?'

'Where are you going?' Crispin always seemed to be asking this.

'Just for a walk. Come *on*, Star!'

'Eleven o'clock, and not a minute later!' Dodo called out after them.

'Yeah, yeah,' replied Jade unconvincingly.

Dodo cried. He sensed rather than saw it. 'What does she mean, "sort out your relationship"?'

'I don't know. I should ignore it, if I were you. Have some more wine. She's angry with herself for behaving badly. She's fed up with us. It's pretty boring going on holiday with your parents. That's all it is. We should have let her go camping with her friends.'

'We should not. God knows what would have happened then.'

'Do you think she's still a virgin?' he asked casually.

Dodo's face shone with tears and surprise. Under the crude

55

red and green Christmas tree lights she looked positively ill. 'Of course. What makes you think otherwise?'

'Oh, I don't. I just wondered.'

'She won't be for long, though, if she goes on like this. I'm worried about her, Crispin.'

'Yes.'

'Is that all you can say?'

'What do you want me to say?'

Dodo started crying again, this time noisily.

'Shush. Calm down, old girl. You've probably overdone it in the sun. Jade's all right. This behaviour of hers is perfectly normal. I was like that at her age. You probably were, too.'

'I was not,' she snuffled.

'Well. Come on, let's go back to the hotel and have a drink by the bar.'

'But what do you think they're *doing*, Crispin?' she persisted as they stumbled down the now unlit path between the river and the road back to the hotel. 'You've seen the way Turkish men react to them. They can't go anywhere without being asked out. I'm sure there are drugs here, too. Oh my God, perhaps we should get the police.'

'I think you've got sunstroke.' He examined her in the light of the Hotel Rhapsody Palas reception. 'You do look rather red. Why don't you go straight to bed? I'll see if I can rustle you up a cup of tea.'

'Oh, Crispin! But what about the girls?'

'I'll stay up for them. I'll make sure they're in, I promise.'

He led her, still crying, to their room. He turned the bed down. 'Shall I run you a bath?'

'We've only got a shower.'

'Oh yes. Well, I'll go and hunt the tea, then.'

Across the other side of the pool, Kizi Demir was dispensing the usual post-dinner drinks. 'Do you think you could do me a brandy and a cup of tea?'

Kizi's impeccably professional face registered no surprise at all. 'Of course, Mr Delancey.'

'The brandy's for me, the tea's for my wife. She's overdone the sun. It's the English remedy. I expect you see that quite a lot here, don't you?'

'Shall I take the tea to your room, Mr Delancey?'

'No, I'll take it. Keep the brandy, I'm coming back for it.'

Dodo was asleep. He put the tea down very quietly, and crept back to the bar.

Kizi pushed the brandy towards him. Crispin settled comfortably on a bar stool. Lisa Upton appeared from somewhere behind him resplendent in a tight cerise silk dress and high-heeled white slingbacks. 'I suppose you haven't seen our Kelly or our Simon, have you?'

Crispin took a swig of his brandy. 'Nope. 'Fraid not.'

'Your girls gone to bed, have they?'

'Nope,' he said again. 'My wife's gone to bed and my girls have gone out on the town.'

Lisa opened her mouth to say something, but thought better of it. 'Goodnight, then,' she said, bringing the heels of her slingbacks sharply together as she turned away from him.

Crispin looked at Kizi Demir, who was polishing glasses. 'Got any cigarettes, Kizi?' Kizi put a packet of cigarettes and a lighter wordlessly in front of him. 'You watch all this, don't you, Kizi?'

Kizi nodded, and continued with his polishing.

'You watch it all, and you notice things, and you do this

week after week, year after year with hundreds of us, and think
how stupid we all are.'

'Not at all.'

'What's the unemployment rate in Turkey these days?'

'Nineteen per cent.'

'So a good job's hard to get.'

'It is.'

'Is this a good job, Kizi?'

'It is a good job, Mr Delancey.' Kizi has had it for five years.
He works here from March through to October every year,
and then from October to February he goes as head waiter to
a ski resort in the mountains. He sends 50 per cent of his wages
home to his parents and six brothers and sisters. His father is
crippled by rheumatism. For seventeen days at the end of February each year Kizi goes home. In his village in the eastern
Anatolian plain there is a young woman called Zephra Saphaz
whom Kizi will marry in two springs' time. Kizi is a hard
worker and a very determined young man. He has a degree in
politics and history and in his spare time he's doing research
for his Ph.D., the subject of which is the development of
tourism in Turkey and its economic, political and religious
implications. When he's got his Ph.D., he'll be able to get a
job at a university where he'll teach history as it should be
taught.

'I bet you think we're all crazy,' incited Crispin.

'Not at all, Mr Delancey.' Kizi was not to be incited. But
it's true he does not respect many of the people he has to
serve at the Hotel Rhapsody Palas. They are such hedonists –
all they want is an unprincipled good time. But there's no place
for a good time when half the world is suffering in chains and
poverty. Moreover, these people seem to have no proper hold

over their children. There is no discipline; moral values are lacking. Love and sex are confused. Family values and pleasure are different things; they may coincide, but this has to be worked for; no one is handed a strong family on a plate. Family ties are the core of a good society. 'Excuse me.' Kizi turned away to serve another client.

Crispin drew sharply on his cigarette. Meg Shaw was standing beside him. 'I'll have a glass of white wine, please, Kizi,' she said quietly. Her voice was melodious, like the hum of a honey bee.

'Put it on my bill, Kizi,' instructed Crispin, in the manner of a Hollywood movie.

'That's all right, thanks, I'd rather pay for it myself. Cheers!' She raised her wine glass to him. 'I hear you braved the mud baths yesterday.' Her head with its delicious crinkle-cut buttery hair was outlined against a cloud of pink geraniums in a pot by the pool, and by the navy blue night sky with the lights of Karput sparkling in the distance. The pink of her lips matched the geraniums. Crispin felt breathless, as though time had stopped.

'What? Oh yes, we did. It was all a bit of a mistake, really. And you, what have you been doing?'

She told him about Ephesus, about the avenue of mulberry trees which guides you there, about the marble street, about the brothel of the Baths of Scolastica, and about standing with her knowledgeable son in the Great Theatre back-shadowed by Mount Pion.

'He's an unusual boy, your Aaron. I mean his interest in serious things is unusual at that age.'

'Oh, he can be a normal teenager, too.' Meg laughed.

'What does Aaron's father do?'

'Why don't you ask me what I do?'

'Fair enough. What do you do?'

'I'm a social worker. It's a good conversation stopper. Why am I a social worker?'

'I wasn't going to ask.'

'And I wasn't going to say.'

'It must be a worthwhile job, though.' Crispin contrasted it with his own, which seemed, especially at this distance and in his current alienated state, rather pointless.

'Must it? Well, from time to time I suppose it is. On balance.' Meg sipped her wine looking at the slow-moving light-embossed river Dinacek and thought about her clients in their damp, cold flats in North Acton with their failed elevators and dog excrement and graffiti on the stairways, and inside the tacky, smelly carpets and cheap take-away food and abuse of children by adults and adults of one another, all in the name of love and the family.

'There's not a lot anyone can do,' she said at last.

'What do you mean, Meg?'

It's the first time he's used her name. It feels to both of them, though more to him than to her, as though he's committed an act of intimacy.

'You want to find out about me, don't you? That's why you asked me about Aaron's father.'

'Well, I . . . well, yes.'

She touched him lightly on the hand. 'That's all right, I'm not complaining. Why should I complain? You're an attractive man. We're on holiday.' She laughed.

Crispin pointed to a table by the river, laid with clean linen and cutlery for breakfast. 'Can I buy you a drink now?'

At ten past eleven, Jade and Star Delancey came back, as

instructed, to the hotel. They found their mother asleep with a cold cup of tea by her bed and their father courting Meg Shaw by the river. Crispin was too occupied with the conversation to notice either the time or the two girls the other side of the floodlit swimming pool.

'I suppose this is what he means by sorting out the relationship,' muttered Jade grimly. 'Come on, Star, we're not needed here.'

The sign outside said 'Sweet Sixteen', and added 'If you are 18 or over come in and have a fun.' Inside, there was a sixties-style juke box next to a malfunctioning pinball game. An old tape of the Rolling Stones was playing loudly, imposing a clash of cultures which reinforced that of the dark-skinned young men eyeing the pale young women and men from the other Karput tourist hotels. All the local young women were safely locked up at home, which is how Kizi Demir would treat his own daughters when he had them.

At a large round table overlooking a patch of the river a kilometre or so upstream of the one their father and Meg Shaw were looking at, Jade and Star Delancey sat down with Kelly and Simon Upton and Joshua Holbeach. They ordered Coke. A joint of hash was circulating. The other side of the Delancey girls were Yusuf and Celik, the two young men who had been generous with their mud. Jade and Star were doing their best to ignore them. 'I think those Turkish dudes are quite fierce,' said Kelly, giggling. 'Don't you just love their little moustaches!'

'This is a kinda dumb place,' remarked Joshua. 'Doncha think, girls?' Inhaling deeply on the joint, he surveyed them across the table. Of the three, Jade was the one he fancied. She'd got a nicely supercilious look about her. Her eyes were always angry, and her back was like a board – he liked good posture in a girl. He'd got no sense of Star yet. But Kelly was the one who was making eyes at him. Mind you, she probably made eyes at everything in trousers. She reminded him a bit of Sigourney Weaver in *Alien*. Good bone structure. 'Aren't your mummies and daddies looking for you?'

'What the hell!' said Kelly flippantly.

What about her brother? He doesn't want the kid sucking up to him. That's what they usually do at that age. 'How old are you, kid?'

'Thirteen.'

'I suppose no one's looking for you, then?' Jade flashed her eyes wonderfully at Joshua.

'My ma yes, my pa no. He's given up on me. Says I'm out of control.'

'Are you?' asked Star curiously.

'I don't like doing what I'm told.'

'So what *do* you like doing?'

'That's a leading question, my girl. It's more a question of what I don't. I don't fancy school much. Or home, come to that. Mostly I just hang around with my friends. We have a drink, take a little acid or a few Es, play a little music, screw around . . .'

'Sounds boring,' said Jade curtly.

'To you, maybe, to me, no. "I seek an inheritance incorruptible, undefiled and that fadeth not away; and it is laid up in heaven, and safe there, to be bestowed, at the time appointed, on them that diligently seek it." But I don't, not yet. Christian in *Pilgrim's Progress*. Bunyan's a hero of mine. He was what they called a ne'er-do-well in his youth. Like me.'

'So you do *go* to school?'

'No, I read books. You can read without going to school. Better, maybe. You lot want a drink?'

'Don't mind if I do,' said Kelly, pushing her glass forward. It's a phrase she's heard her mother use.

'Rum and Coke, okay?'

Kelly nodded.

Joshua fetched the drinks. The Turkish youths had started on the Delancey girls again. A few people were dancing under the trees, which had coloured lights strung in them like the restaurant where earlier this evening the Delancey family ate their strained supper. Jade and one of the youths got up to dance. After the first few bars she came back to the table and kicked off her DMs. She had major holes in her tights, through which interesting little pieces of flesh beckoned.

He drained his glass. Okay, if you can't beat 'em, join 'em. 'I don't like dancing, but maybe they need showing a trick or two. Come on, girlie' – he pulled Kelly up by the arm – 'it'll take the two of us.'

He was an amazing dancer. All his joints seemed to bend lots of ways and his arms were like liquid snakes in the air. Kelly was feeling quite intoxicated, even though she'd had only one rum. It was hot dancing, so she took off her t-shirt. Underneath she wore a short black vest. He could see her nipples, hard and small, through it. Jade took off her shirt, too; but she was wearing a kind of half blouse, though her midriff was bare. 'Hey, you,' he said, catching an image in his mind, 'can you belly dance?'

'Of course not,' she said.

'Belly dance?' said one of the Turkish youths. 'I show you belly dance.' He began moving his hips in a different way and

Jade copied him, and Joshua copied her, and pretty soon they were all doing it. People started clapping to the rhythm. Star and Simon weren't dancing, but they came out and stood under the trees, clapping loudly. Everybody was smiling. 'This is a bit more like it, isn't it, girls!' said Joshua. He took Jade by the middle and put his hands on her warm white flesh. Her eyes focused aggressively on him. 'Come on, lovey, I'm not doing anything. Just dance with me.' After a bit she started to relax. He picked her up just a little the first time. She was surprised. People shouted. And then more the next time. The dancing got wilder. A boatload of fishermen rowing past in the black water stopped and started singing in Turkish. The Turkish youths roared with laughter. The other one got hold of Star, and was whirling her round and round. Simon went to the bar and got himself a drink. He came back and sat under the trees watching. He was a little frightened now – he'd seen the time, it was nearly two o'clock.

Back downstream in the Hotel Rhapsody Palas, Crispin Delancey and Meg Shaw sat under the stars drinking coffee. Everyone else had gone to bed. Kizi Demir wanted to turn out the floodlights in the swimming pool, and finish for the night; he'd been planning to write a long letter to Zephra, but that would have to wait for another night now.

Crispin and Meg got up. 'I'll walk you to your room.' Crispin had difficulty standing, and even more difficulty walking straight. Everything he'd done today was catching up with him, from the cycling to the boozing in Kracjek with Martin Holbeach, and all the arguments and conversations and alcohol of the last few hours. He laughed happily. 'I've really enjoyed myself tonight,' he said, 'talking to you. You can't imagine how good it's been.' She had to take his arm to steer him safely away from the edge of the pool. 'That's right,' he giggled, 'we don't want to fall in, do we!'

'Shush. This is my room. I'm going in,' she said firmly. 'Thank you for the drinks.'

'I want to kiss you,' Crispin admitted weakly.

'I don't think that would be a good idea.'

'A cuddle then?'

Before she could say anything, he'd got his arms round her; her nose was pressed against his shoulder. It smelled clean and fresh and masculine. It brought back memories. Her proximity provoked him, and he reached for her face, tipping it gently towards his with a finger lightly under her chin, so her skin caught the full whiteness of the moonlight. While he was involved in this face-tipping exercise, an odd memory occurred to him: the feeling of Martin Holbeach's smooth white back under his creamy hands in the shade of a cypress tree.

In the middle of the kiss, Lisa Upton came out of the room next to Meg's, and Crispin was so surprised he lost his balance and fell over into one of Suleyman's carefully planted rose bushes.

Lisa helped Meg to pick Crispin up. 'Caught in the act,' he said, like a schoolboy. 'You won't tell . . .'

'There's one born every minute, isn't there?' said Lisa to Meg, who seemed to understand what she meant.

The noise woke Dodo up. She put on the light and saw the cold tea and felt a rush of love for Crispin, and drank it. But where was he? She got out of bed and padded to the door in her thin flower-sprigged Laura Ashley nightgown.

'Crispin!'

There were some figures in the blackness.

'Coming, darling!'

'What's going on?'

Lisa Upton explained: 'I came out to see if I could find Kelly and Simon. I thought they were in bed asleep, but Stevie just woke me up. He had a bad dream and they weren't there.'

Dodo was terribly sympathetic. 'Oh dear. I'll go and see if the girls know anything.' She was back in a minute, shaking. 'They're not here, either. My God, where are they?'

Unfortunately Crispin's condition made him a less than efficient sorter-out of this particular mess. Derrick Upton took charge. He decided they must mount a search. Crispin thought this a bit unnecessary, as Karput was probably not half as dangerous as Hampstead, and they'd all drift back to the hotel eventually anyway. But Dodo's worries urged them on. Derrick located Kizi, who was doing his final locking up before going to bed, and enlisted his help. Where would an assortment of disenchanted pleasure-seeking young people have gone? There were three nightclubs in the town, Kizi informed them. He fetched a map and marked their location. He offered to accompany Derrick. Derrick had a suspicion that Joshua Holbeach was at the bottom of this, so he knocked at the Holbeaches' door. Martin opened it, wrapped in a towel. 'I'm sorry to disturb you, but our children are missing. We wondered if your son knew where they were.'

'Jesus! Is that why you've got me up? He probably does. But it won't help you, because he's not likely to be here either. He's rarely back before four these days. I've had enough of it, myself. I should go back to bed if I were you.'

Derrick and Kizi set out together. The streets were mostly deserted, and the minaret of the mosque rose in a sea of stars as though trying to make a moral point of some kind. Around the base of the mosque, thin Turkish cats raged and whined, mangling last night's restaurant pickings, and a taut coupling or two took place in the low scrub at the back. Derrick Upton and Kizi Demir strode out towards the Musicquarium, the first of Kizi's list of nightclubs. Outside it was cool, with a languid breeze coming off the river, but inside the Musicquarium the air was full of body smells and the sour odour of undigested alcohol. 'I'll kill them when I find them!' pronounced Derrick, as he went inside, but no killing would take place, as they weren't there.

'The next one's down here, Mr Upton.' Kizi pointed down a dead-end street leading off the main square; it was in the direction of the man kicking the football. 'Mari Boncuf,' said the neon sign: 'Café bar club. 7-up. Pepsi.'

But this one was locked. 'I forgot,' said Kizi, 'excuse me. The manager, he is getting married in Izmir tomorrow.' He was actually marrying a distant relative of Zephra's. She and Kizi had been invited to the wedding but Kizi couldn't get time off, and Zephra wouldn't go without him.

'I'm afraid the last one is the other way, back past the hotel.'

Derrick marched on. They passed the turning to the hotel and walked down a road which was sprinkled with 'Pansiyon' signs: 'Nar Pansiyon', 'Zakhum Pansiyon', 'Adem Pansiyon', 'Hot water and breakfast', 'Heir spreck mann deutsch'. 'If they're not at any of the nightclubs,' said Derrick, 'where would they be? Bloody good holiday, this!' he stamped on. 'I'll throttle our Kelly, it'll be her who put both of them up to this. Ah, what have we here, then?'

Round the next corner came Joshua, Jade, Star, Kelly, Simon, Yusuf and Celik. They were strung out across the road like fairy lights. Joshua had his arm round Jade, Celik was hand in hand with Star, Yusuf and Kelly had their arms round each other's waists. Only Simon walked alone, unsteadily, eating a large chocolate icecream on a stick.

Derrick stood in the middle of the road, his legs apart in a strident, patriarchal pose. 'Where the hell have you all been?' he thundered. 'I suppose this is your idea of a good time. Well, it's not mine. I suppose you think you're being very clever. Well, I've got news for you. You're bloody not. You're a load of thick inconsiderate yobbos. You don't deserve the time of day. Yes, I know only two of you are mine, but what I say goes for the whole bloody lot of you!'

By the end of this speech, there were quite a few people watching. Some of the Pansiyon owners even came out to make sure that there was nothing interesting going on.

Derrick Upton yanked Kelly by the neck of her t-shirt and Simon by the hand with the chocolate icecream in it. 'And who are these two, might I ask?' he asked, pointing at Yusuf and Celik.

Kizi felt some sense of camaraderie with his compatriots. He talked to them quickly in Turkish, advising them to make themselves scarce, which they did.

Derrick marched Kelly and Simon back to the hotel. Star and Jade Delancey grinned nervously at Kizi. 'I'm sorry,' said Star, 'have we kept you up?' Kizi raised his eyes to Allah. 'It's quite funny, really,' said Star after a bit, 'isn't it?' No one laughed.

Behind them all loped Joshua Holbeach with bent shoulders and scowling, not unlike his father.

FOUR

Turtle Beach

'I blame the Holbeach boy,' said Derrick Upton to Lisa over breakfast, which he was filming, as they were on their own, and she had tucked a couple of yellow roses in her hair. 'It's outrageous,' he observed powerlessly. 'It shouldn't be allowed.'

'Well, how are you going to stop it?'

Derrick was silent. 'You'll have to talk to the boy's mother, Lisa.'

'What good will that do?'

'We've got another two and a half weeks in this place. That's seventeen more nights when whatsisname Holbeach can repeat last night's performance. My health won't stand for it.' He passed a hand across his forehead. Looking in the mirror this morning, he had understood for the first time what looking pale under your suntan meant. 'I've got that big job at Withams on when I get back. I need a proper holiday, Lisa.'

Crispin and Dodo Delancey weren't too happy, either. Crispin had a hangover and Dodo had twigged that he'd been doing some serious drinking last night – drinking which interfered with his promise to check that the girls had come back to the hotel when they were supposed to. This added insult to injury, in view of his misdemeanours earlier in the day. 'What kind of father are you?' she demanded. 'Anything could have happened to them. You wouldn't have known. It's all words and no actions with you, Crispin. Always has been. You live in a world of fantasy most of the time. All you care about is number one. Sometimes I wonder why you don't just piss off and leave us alone. We'd be better off without you. At least I'd know where I stand then! And this is supposed to be a bloody holiday!'

Crispin, with a sheet over his face to cut out the light, remembered Martin Holbeach's remark by the side of the lake, and wondered if this was the menopause. If so, he'd rather have good old PMT any day. He was struck by Dodo's allegation that he cared only about himself. But all he cared about at the moment was Meg Shaw: the softness of her skin in the moonlight, the fresh, lavender-ish smell of her glorious crinkly hair; her low, singing voice and gentle laughter, her quiet, sophisticated intelligence. The image of the woman in the golden bikini had been supplanted by another; that of the erotically promising woman in the white dress. The contrast with Dodo was obvious: Dodo's curves were rounded, like cushions; Dodo's face was open, clean, honest, like a desert. Meg's face was a complex, delicate, wonderfully pretty map of unknown thoughts and emotions. Her bracing blue eyes gave very little away. Her body was like a tonic – small, firm, shapely, brimming with restrained energy.

'Crispin, did you hear what I said?'

'I heard.'

'Aren't you going to say anything?'

'What can I say? You're right. I'm a wimp. And I did get seriously pissed last night. I'm sorry. Of course I'm sorry. You haven't got any paracetamol, have you?'

By the time Dodo got to the pool there was only one sunbed left. Next to it were a couple of honeymooners, and the Uptons

– one of the Uptons; for Lisa could be seen at a table by the river earnestly locked in verbal combat with Sandy Holbeach. Derrick was sunning his back.

Dodo noticed he had his video camera under his chair. She could just imagine him and Lisa in their modern semi in Chigwell setting up their holiday video for friends and neighbours to watch. But they probably all did the same. Jade had been at her for one of those. 'You can get them for five hundred pounds at Dixon's. I want to be a film-maker. It's creative, you should be pleased.'

'You wanted to be a palaeontologist last week.'

'That was last week.'

At the table by the river, Lisa Upton was finding Sandy Holbeach something of a puzzle. She had an air of disordered vagueness, as though she couldn't make out what she was supposed to be doing. But it was difficult to square this with her two occupations – those of mother and professional therapist. Her oddly ranged family suggested either humanitarian motives or a fairly powerful drive towards motherhood. But if Sandy was desperate to be a mother, it was hard to understand why she seemed so permanently miserable about it.

Lisa and Sandy were drinking coffee, but Sandy had ordered a brandy 'to keep up her strength'. She was defensive about her son. 'Josh is having a hard time working himself out right now,' she told Lisa Upton. 'What teenager doesn't? But it's been especially difficult for him with Primrose and Freddie being adopted. We've only had Freddie a year, and he hasn't really settled in yet. Joshua feels displaced from being the centre of the family. He has a very high IQ, but his self-esteem hasn't caught up. He's angry with me for not being able to give him a brother or sister naturally. I had a hysterectomy ten years ago, you see. The fibroids filled a bucket.' Her eyes brimmed with tears.

'That's all very well,' said Lisa, mindful of the reason she sat down here in the first place, 'and I'm sorry about your womb. But Joshua does seem to be, well, rather out of control. The problem is, he's leading the other children on.'

Sandy pointed out that this problem belonged to the other parents.

Lisa was confused by this. 'Yes, but we're all in this together, aren't we?' She tried again, appealing to empty commonalities, despite her intuitive dislike of wet north London mothers who've got nothing better to do than be occupied with identity problems. 'We're stuck here in this' – she looked around her as though she were on a rubbish tip – 'little bit of paradise together, and we're all supposed to be having a holiday. We've got to do our best to make it work, haven't we? My Derrick needs a holiday,' she added, remembering his remark about Withams, 'and I expect your husband's in the same position. Of course it's not really a holiday for us women, is it, not when the children are there. But at least we don't have to cook every night. Maybe we ought to, well, work out some joint rules about things like what time they're supposed to be back here at night, and letting us know where they are, and that sort of thing? Then we could have a meeting and put those to the children.' This had been Derrick's idea. He was a strong trade unionist, and even though Lisa didn't approve of the more solidly working-class aspects of this activity (her own under-standing of matters of class defied easy interpretation), the idea of a consensus seemed a good one.

'It wouldn't work.'

'How do you know?'

'Teenagers don't respond to rules. You have to discuss things with them, bring them round to your point of view gradually.'

'How do you know?' asked Lisa again.

'From my professional work. I'm a therapist. I specialize in adolescents.' Sandy looked melancholy. 'I'll try talking to Josh, but I can't promise anything. You see, relations with his father have practically broken down, and that's a very important element in this situation. You see, the father represents discipline, strength, order . . .'

'Come on, girls!' Martin Holbeach strode over. 'It's drinkies time. What can I get you?'

'Oh yes,' said Sandy vaguely. 'Are Primrose and Freddie about? I'll have another brandy, I think.'

'Freddie wants to go in the pool. Primrose wants to go shopping. And you, Mrs Upton, what can I get you?'

In their darkened room, Jade and Star Delancey came to consciousness as the maid first banged on the door and then entered noisily with her cleaning tools.

Star sat up. 'Oh, I'm sorry, we'll be up in a minute.' She went to the bathroom, steering a hazardous course round the half-eaten food, the Pepsi-Cola cans, the plastic cassette boxes, and six pairs of DMs. Then she lifted up a corner of the curtain and looked out across their tiny patio to the grass and the swimming pool, and the bar and the river and the granite wall of the mountain opposite, riddled with the holes and columns of the Lycian rock tombs. Why anyone would want to get themselves buried up there was beyond her. How could you get dead bodies up there anyway, let alone carry all that masonry in such a crumbly, inhospitable place? Between this nicely disorganized room and the screwy rock tombs, Star could see her mother talking to Joshua Holbeach's mother and to Kelly and Simon's mother. No doubt about last night. Joshua's father was mincing towards them affecting to be a waiter with a tray of drinks balanced on the palm of his left hand. Her mother was wearing her white bikini. She looked particularly yukky in this, and more so when sitting, as this allowed the flesh on her waist, abdomen and hips to settle in seriously offensive circles. The fact that the circles were now brown did nothing to recommend them. Star drew her own stomach in and pushed her chest out through her t-shirt. She ran her hand round her waist and hips, checking their dimensions.

She got back into bed and watched Jade sleeping. She envied Jade's anger and determination: Jade always seemed to know what she wanted. Did Jade want Joshua Holbeach? Star thought she did. Joshua certainly wanted Jade. Star closed her eyes and remembered last night: the smoke rings, the relaxing effect of the crude hash-hash, the cutting taste of the vodka, the darkly focused attentions of Yusuf and Celik; the way Joshua had sprawled across a chair, using the table as a knee prop, and seeming to be so at home there; the high bright lights, the rhythmic din of the music; Kelly Upton's long graceful neck and her pert face angled towards Joshua; and then, later, dancing by the river under the strangely shaped trees with the mosquitoes trying to bite the moving targets of their jerky wrists and ankles; and the warm, silky air flowing all around, with the odd persistent jarring hum of the cicadas, and the living scents of flowers matched to their colours in heady heat and depth. Rather than feeling herself to be part of this scene, Star saw herself there in it, from the vantage point of someone circling in the air overhead and casually noting what was going on. She had a sense of emotional disconnection – an ability to cut herself off from the feelings she knew, somewhere deep inside, she had.

She'd tried to get Jade to go back to the hotel earlier. But Jade would have none of it, and Star hadn't wanted to walk back on her own. She didn't really understand why her mother had been so upset, though; it was as if she'd thought they'd been killed or something. What could have happened to them in a tiny place like this, where the young men had never even stopped wearing flared trousers or listening to Cliff Richard? Maybe her mother had been upset about something else. Maybe it was because she'd seen her father talking to that woman. Star got back out of bed and let herself out of the room by the door that faced the front of the hotel rather than the swimming pool. She crossed the cold marble floor of the reception area and walked down the corridor lining the rooms and the riverside. This enabled her to get to her parents' room without her mother seeing. The door was open. The room was dark, and her father was apparently asleep. 'Dad?' She stood over the double bed looking at him. 'Dad?'

'Star! What is it?'

'Are you all right, Dad?'

At her question, he was fully awake. 'Of course I am, my love. Why, what's the matter?' When she was little she would have got into bed with him, but she was fifteen and he was naked. He patted the side of the bed. 'Sit down and tell me.'

Star sat down with her back to her father. 'You know last night?'

Crispin affirmed that he did.

'Were you furious with us?'

Crispin tried to remember. 'I was cross. You should have

75

come back when you were supposed to. But I wasn't as cross as your mother.'

'What were you doing last night, Dad?'

What did she mean? 'What do you mean, Star?'

'Mum said you were pissed. Who did you get pissed with?'

'Myself,' he said quickly, too quickly.

'Oh.'

'What's wrong with that? Oh, I know I shouldn't drink, but we are on holiday.'

Star understood her father had something to hide. 'Can we go somewhere today, Dad?'

'You mean apart from to the swimming pool and back?'

'Yes. It's boring here.'

'I'll talk to your mother.'

'Why can't *you* decide?'

'Oh come on, Star, you know she's the boss.' He flung off the sheet and then, remembering his nakedness, flung it back on again.

After lunch, which nobody ate much of, except Jade, whose appetite for food was like her appetite for life – insatiable – the Delanceys discussed where they should go. Dodo consulted the guidebook. 'What about the Roman bridge at Yuvlik? Or the thermal baths: "The water has properties that are of benefit in cases of neuralgia, neuritis, rheumatismal ailments, skin disorders, and calcification. The radioactivity is 98.3",' she read.

'No, I don't think so,' said Star. 'We don't want to be radioactive, thank you very much. And I heard one of the bird-watchers saying the other day that the government's been trying to close them down.'

Jade said she had been talking to Portia Dunkerley, who wanted to come somewhere with them. Portia was tired of visits to historical sites, and Jade had every sympathy. Dodo said they couldn't take Portia anywhere without offering to take Kelly and Simon and maybe Stevie as well. She said we're not taking everybody, particularly not Joshua Holbeach, and particularly in view of last night. Jade said what's it got to do with last night? Dodo said everything, and you're grounded for the next five days. No going anywhere outside the hotel. Jade said what does outside the hotel mean? Dodo said don't be pedantic, Jade. Jade said she wasn't. She was only trying to suss out what the rules really were so she could act accordingly.

Star said, 'Why don't we hire lots of boats and all go to the beach?'

Crispin groaned at the thought of all the organization that would be required for this, though it did occur to him that 'all' would include the woman in the white dress. 'Good idea,' he said. Then another good idea struck him. 'Maybe your mother would like an afternoon off? I could take you. We could take the boats further if you like,' he went on, really enthused by his idea, 'and have a look at the caves round the corner of the bay at Gochek. I've heard they're very good for snorkelling.'

Star gave him a very odd, firm look.

'Oh well, perhaps not. We'll do Daddy's treat another time.'

After about an hour of complicated organizing, in which the prime movers were Dodo and Star, with some help from Kizi, who was interested in getting as many of them as possible off his hands for the afternoon, the hotel boat set off with the Delanceys plus Portia Dunkerley plus Aaron Shaw plus Kelly and Simon and Stevie and Lisa Upton. To Crispin's great dismay, Meg Shaw had gone shopping with Wilma Blake. Not only was he dismayed that she wouldn't be coming, he was also quite upset to hear her name associated with such a lowly activity. Crispin remembered Meg was a social worker. That must account for it.

They went the other way this time; the boat passed the southern side of the hotel, and became one of the noises that Crispin and Dodo would have heard from their room had they been there. There were a lot of boats about, coming and going from Turtle Beach. 'They're called *Caretta carettas,*' said Portia Dunkerley knowledgeably. 'They're loggerhead turtles. This is one of only two places in the world they still breed. Daddy says there are more than four hundred nests here every year.' Jade stared at her. Portia carried a little green and red holdall with her swimming things in it. She wore a plain check cotton frock and sandals. She could be five years younger than the other girls, not just several.

The beach had a kind of mooring platform to which a row of boats were tied. They all trooped off. A huge expanse of white sand greeted them, dotted with hundreds of people in deckchairs with coloured umbrellas and boys keenly collecting inflated sums of money. Beyond all this private enterprise, the Aegean Sea rose like a frilled glass plate, its waves gently mixing with the warm sand and the bodies of the few of its visitors who had decided to get wet.

The women were organizing deckchairs. Portia had dropped her holdall and was making a sandcastle with Stevie Upton. Jade and Star were surveying the local talent and the prospect of bars on the horizon. Kelly and Simon were helping the women find deckchairs. Only Aaron Shaw stood still, contemplatively, looking at the ocean.

'Impressive, isn't it?'

'The sea always is.' The boy looked at Crispin for a moment, and then away.

'Are you going to swim?'

'Oh yes. That's what we've come for, haven't we?'

The women were derobing. Jade and Star and Kelly were peeling off their t-shirts and sundresses. Stevie had been lured from his sandcastle to have pink wings put on. Portia was looking round for somewhere to change.

'You'll have to do it here, dear. With a towel around you.'

It was unbelievably contorting to watch. She emerged eventually. 'What do I do with my glasses, Mrs Delancey? Mummy said I'm to keep them on, but I can't swim in them, can I?'

'Give them to me,' offered Crispin. 'I'll stay and look after everything and go in later.'

'Would you mind, darling?'

'That's very nice of you,' said Lisa, 'here's my purse.'

He also got the girls' Walkmen, assorted bags of sun lotion and seaside reading material, and Stevie's Nintendo Gameboy. One of the keen inflationary beach lads came to collect money. Crispin counted out the dirty flaccid lire. He smiled at the boy, who was dazzlingly pretty in nothing but a pair of knee-long indigo cycling shorts. A scene from *Death in Venice* came to mind; the ageing, made-up Mahler, seated stiffly in a deckchair by the pale lido watching with cavernous melancholy eyes for the beautiful young lad in his striped bathing suit. I'm getting old, thought Crispin. Misleading images are attacking me. What I need is a good dose of reality. He forced his eyes to focus on the figures in the sea. Dodo and Lisa were holding Stevie's hands, swinging him across the baby waves as he and Dodo had once done with the girls. Instead of reality, Crispin was savaged by a distant image which imposed its violent sweetness upon him: Jade as a small child, on first being taken to the sea, the North Sea on a quiet June day in Suffolk, England, as different from here as could be imagined – and running straight in with innocent delight and having to be chased and restrained before she got out of her depth. Dodo had been holding Star, a baby of four months, so he did the running. He had caught Jade and lifted her to the sky and felt her clean young limbs awash with the sea and the pure joy of living, and it had been one of those moments which imprints itself to be summoned up at will when living has become what it most often is, a complicated, poorly splendoured thing.

Out in the Aegean Sea, Simon Upton was still wading in, and Aaron Shaw was swimming steadily out and away from the babble and noise. Kelly and the Delancey sisters were riding the waves and shouting to each other, and Kelly was going on a few forays under the surface to see what could be seen. She was coming up with all sorts of stories about skeletons and jelly-fish in order to drive the others to a shrieking teenage girl hysteria. Portia Dunkerley had thrown herself with gusto into the waves, but was only on the edges of this game and so resignedly swam away in the direction of what without her glasses could only be a misty blue blur.

It must be nice and cool in the sea. Crispin took his own t-shirt off and lay back. If he allowed his mind to wander, he knew what it'd do; it'd fix on the persona of Meg Shaw and plan all kinds of illicit expeditions they wouldn't go on together. A secret trip into the lemon groves in the hills above Karput, where peasants in unspoiled villages would watch them pass like creatures from another planet? A midnight flit in the night-clubs of Marmaris? Perhaps they could sneak off for a few hours and whisk a *dolmus* up to the freshwater lake which Kizi had told him was the most beautiful and wild place he had ever seen? Or maybe a journey on a magic carpet far above and beyond all this, to some land of the imagination where rules about bodies and what could be done with them weren't allowed to intrude?

Crispin hadn't though much about his body since he was a young man, but he was becoming increasingly conscious of it now. He'd never considered himself a particularly sexual man. At his vegetarian boarding school in Hatfield, he'd been frightened of girls, and after a troublesome encounter with one Angela Carrington, who later married a lord, even more frightened. From this he'd been rescued by Dodo, whose calm dogged persistence in the face of (his) failure ultimately triumphed. After that Dodo had been enough for him. More or less. There had been moments when he'd grappled with theories about having other women, but they'd always been vanquished by the problematic reality of getting them. Fortunately Crispin had never realized how attractive he was to women. A psychiatrist might have blamed his low self-esteem or insufficiently developed sense of masculinity on his troubled relations with his father; but to most people it was simply modesty.

Crispin and Dodo's sex life had been at the once a week or fortnight (depending on the season), ten minutes of foreplay, him on top of her, and straight to sleep afterwards level for many years. This was, he understood, how it is for most couples. It seemed to be enough for Dodo. At least she hadn't complained about it. Crispin wondered how it was with Meg Shaw. Did she have sex? If so, with whom?

Crispin's thoughts were interrupted by shouts from the sea. Portia had swum out of her depth in her journey towards Greece. Dodo had struck out after her, but she wasn't a vigorous swimmer. Jade, who was, had followed, but both were some distance away. Crispin stood up and started taking his trousers off, afflicted with nightmare thoughts about returning Portia-less to the hotel to confront the professors Dunkerley. But it was Aaron Shaw who quietly and powerfully swam to the spot and rescued Portia, delivering her on to the sand in front of Crispin. She was quite beside herself, shaking and crying and looking terribly white. Aaron laid her down and pushed a heap of towels under her head. 'I did a first aid course at school,' he explained.

'Don't tell Mummy and Daddy,' pleaded Portia pitiably, struggling for breath, 'they'll be terribly cross. I'm supposed to be a good swimmer, and I should have kept my glasses on.'

Dodo tried to comfort her. 'You are a good swimmer, dear, you just went a bit too far and got frightened.'

'I can't see anything,' she moaned. 'I want my glasses.'

'Give her her glasses, Crispin,' instructed Dodo.

Crispin searched, but couldn't find them.

'I put them in my purse for safe-keeping,' said Lisa. But they couldn't find that, either. Eventually they surmised that in the short time Crispin was absent at the water's edge someone had taken it.

Portia's sobs turned into an enormous wail. Everyone tried to console her, and then Jade said, 'Oh for God's sake, shut up! You've only lost your bloody glasses. They were pretty horrible anyway.'

Crispin bought them all icecreams, and looked at his watch: five thirty. Aaron's mother ought to be back from her shopping trip by now. Would she wear her white dress tonight? At least the Delanceys would have to eat in the hotel, after last night's row under the coloured lights.

The return trip was subdued. When they got to the Hotel Rhapsody Palas, the sun was about to slip behind the granite of the rock tombs, and the professors Dunkerley awaited them by the river's edge, sipping the remains of their late afternoon tea.

FIVE

The Night of the Storm

Over the next couple of days, things quietened down in the Hotel Rhapsody Palas. Several residents had exceeded their roast-by dates round the swimming pool, and were forced to sit inside and think about the paradox of how punishing to one's body a Proper Holiday could be. The blue sky was broken by clouds anyway, and the Welsh bird-watchers arranged a trip to the Mersin delta, where they hoped to find a breeding population of purple gallinules. A sighting of the marbled teal would be a bonus. The two Joans were persuaded to go with them.

Portia's encounters with the sea hadn't diluted her enthusiasm for being a part of what her father referred to as 'the youth club'. Grizelda bore her off to the optician in Karput, a sad underemployed refugee from the north, and got her a new pair of even less flattering glasses. Portia had cottoned on to the fact that the youth club all slept late, and tried to herself, but this was difficult, as she shared a room with her parents. (The Dunkerleys were careful with their money. Ronald had even suggested that the Delanceys should be asked to pay for Portia's new glasses.)

Ronald himself was at a bit of a loose end. Grizelda was making notes for next term's lectures when she wasn't taking Portia to the optician, and when she wasn't doing either of these, she was trying to enter into the holiday spirit by reading Rose Macaulay's *The Towers of Trebizond*. This was, after all, about a group of eccentric English who explored Turkey by means of a camel. Sometimes Ronald thought that in marrying Grizelda he had combined the worst elements of both his parents; his father had been a professor of theology who'd never done anything but work, and his mother was a domestically disorganized artist who'd had a lot of children without really understanding why. Ronald had been off on one or two expeditions of his own – to see the Byzantine ruins on Deysane island and the rock tombs shaped like eagles' nests upriver – but too much exploring in this heat was an uncomfortable business.

Suleyman, the hotel gardener, was making a shady garden on the seafaring side of the hotel for guests to sit in. The Proper Holidays rep had told Mehmet that this would increase the hotel's popularity. Most of the garden was now finished, though some climbing roses were still on order.

Ronald took refuge in the garden, locating himself beneath a yellow Leverkusen rambler with Brice's *The Turkish Coloniz- ation of Anatolia*. The Holbeaches were also there, quarrel- ling about Joshua in low voices. Ronald wasn't interested, and had always had the capacity to cut out extraneous noise. But he did see Kizi bringing Martin Holbeach a shiny cylin- der of paper, and Martin reading it and getting up abruptly and Sandy shrieking at him, 'That's the bloody limit, that is! Don't tell me they can't manage without you, I don't believe it for a minute! It's only an excuse to ignore your responsi- bilities to us. I don't know what you had a bloody family for!'

'Fax from the office,' explained Martin, waving it as he

walked past Ronald's seat. 'The Bosnian conflict. They need advice on the editorial line.'

Ronald nodded. He also couldn't help noticing, when Martin had gone, that Sandy was weeping. Non-interfering in other people's affairs as he was, Ronald was incapable of ignoring a woman's tears. It had been drilled into him by his father, along with other similarly, though less useful, patriarchal adages about gender relations. Ronald migrated from his comfortable seat under the Leverkusen to Sandy's less comfortable one next to a red hybrid musk with the beginnings of blackfly. He put a hand on one of her wet ones. 'Forgive me, I couldn't help but hear. Please don't upset yourself. I'm sure Mr Holbeach doesn't mean to be difficult.'

A painted lady hovered with a rapid whirring of wings on an orange miniature shrub rose. Sandy half-smiled at him behind her tears. 'Thank you for your concern.' She sniffed fiercely, trying to take the effluvia of her tears back inside her head. She wiped her eyes, tucking a stray damp strand of dark hair behind a delicately jewelled ear. It was a beautiful ear, Ronald noticed, with an eye for architectural detail: coral pink, despite the sun, like a seashell fashioned by millennia of the syncopated rhythm of tidal seas and shifting sands and stone. 'Let me order you a coffee or something,' he found himself saying, under the influence of the seashell ear.

Sandy selected another brandy. 'It's not like this at home,' she explained. 'At home we have a girl who comes in four days a week to help with the children. I have a private counselling practice, you see. You wouldn't think it, though, would you, from the state I'm in now?'

'I don't see why we have to be immune from the weaknesses we study,' reflected Ronald, thinking of his own tendency as a professor of history to bury both pleasant and unpleasant things under layers of metaphorical earth. 'Indeed, your own sensitivities must surely make you a better counsellor, not a worse one!'

Why doesn't Martin say such sensible confidence-boosting things to me? Sandy asked herself. With the heightened sensibilities of the moment – this artificial oasis of tourist pleasure, these few acres of historical bougainvillaea-loaded Euro-Asia bounded by different sorts of water on all sides, this ineffable, evanescent time out of time – Ronald Dunkerley knew what Sandy Holbeach was thinking. The two sat for a moment in what would have been a tense silence, had it not been for the continued whirring of the butterfly and dragonfly wings, the swishing of the green river grasses in the wind that blew from the sea, and the sounds of the motorboats passing on the river behind them. Sandy looked at Ronald gratefully, but didn't know what to say. Ronald looked at Sandy, expecting her to say something. Both were rescued by the arrival of Wilma Blake, in a large locally purchased sun-hat and dress sporting green and pink turtles and with a copy of the *Daily Mail* tucked under her arm. 'Good afternoon.' She stomped politely past them with her big handbag to the shadiest spot in the garden, where Suleyman had arranged a special umbrella for her. She came here at regular times: between ten and twelve in the morning and between four and six in the afternoon. In the morning she read a paperback novel from the hotel's own collection – at the moment it was Danielle Steel's *Secrets* – and in the afternoon the *Daily Mail*, which she'd arranged to have delivered to the hotel. In the early mornings before the sun was too hot she went for a walk round Karput, and in the early afternoons she usually slept, though she could be persuaded to go on an expedition, as on the day of the trip to the mud baths. Before dinner she spent an hour or so with Stevie, who was as yet untainted by the wildness of the pubertal Uptons, and still enjoyed reading and playing games, including Happy Families, for which Wilma had an old set of cards her Derrick had played with in his own childhood.

Wilma Blake was seventy-seven. She had been born in 1915, during a war in which her eldest brother and her father had both died; she lost a fiancé, a gentle-eyed stonemason, in the Second World War, and survived all this to marry Bertram Upton, Derrick's father, in 1946. The cottage in Diddington was home to all these memories. Of Evie, Wilma's mother, and the mother of another nine of them, packed like sardines in feather beds dressed in clean garden-smelling white sheets, and brought up to respect each other's different ways and the sameness of the country's, through generation after generation of human foibles: the cycle of the seasons, the wisdom of the black rainfall and the quiet watching eye of the sun; the irascible rooting of invisible brown moles under well-tended fields and gardens; the calving of the cows and the lambing of the sheep; the crowing of the cocks and the strutting of the hens; the golden ripening season of the barley and the corn and the wheat, with poppies dotted round their untidy edges in remembrance of all that spent military blood.

Far from home, Wilma Blake read in the *Daily Mail* about the war in Bosnia. Without looking, she saw the other inmates of the garden: Gareth Barrett, with his swinging binoculars, though he ought to have been out pursuing gallinules; Lisa Upton burying something under a rose bush. (The hotel cat wandered over later and uncovered a nice piece of fish kebab with a crabby paw.) For a while Sandy Holbeach and

Ronald Dunkerley sat on their seat talking in quiet voices; then the dark lank figure of Sandy's eldest came on a hunt for money, after which Sandy left with Joshua, and some minutes later Ronald went too. The honeymooners came and took their seat, sitting with arms intertwined like the knobbly branches of the grapevines growing over the breakfast tables. Wilma Blake sometimes thought she would like to be young again.

The late twenties and early thirties had been a happy time for her. She'd been in service at the Manor House in Wheelam with Lord and Lady Mellor and their brood of four well-heeled youngsters. There'd been a staff of sixteen: butler, under-butler, cook, four kitchenmaids, housekeeper, housemaids, nanny, chauffeur, seamstress, secretary. Miss Willow, Lord Mellor's secretary, had regarded herself as being a cut above the rest of the staff, but she wasn't really. Wilma had worked as a housemaid. She'd been pretty and well-mannered (Evie had seen to that) so Mrs Broxton, the housekeeper, sometimes let her do things which were above her station, like serve sherry the colour of ripening corn to the early dinner guests, or take in Lady Mellor's tea in the morning. Wilma remembered even now the sheen of the daylight on the fine bone-china cup set on its little hand-crocheted pure white doily on the silver tray polished to a high bright gleam by Vera, the silver maid. Lady Mellor's awakenings had been so perfect. Of course she'd slept on her own, all the aristocracy had – it was a wonder, Evie's mother used to say, that anything happened between the sheets at all. Lady Mellor would be lying still in the middle of the big bed with its rose damask quilt and heavy lace curtains, the bed hardly disarranged at all by the night's sleeping, and when Wilma knocked and came in, Lady Mellor would open those amazing lime green eyes of hers – all of a sudden they would be wide open and shining – and sit up in bed, and her cream silk nightgown with the pattern of ground ivy and forget-me-nots embroidered on the front would have scarcely a crease showing, and she would say – it was always the same – 'Help me with the pillows, please, Wilma,' and Wilma did, after first drawing the deep-green brocade curtains to let in the light. The view from Lady Mellor's bedroom was of the carved stone lions at the front of the house. Wilma liked these less than what lay beyond, which she thought then quite the most beautiful sight anyone could hope to see every morning: a green meadow, full of daisies in summertime, edging a clear wild lake over which birds flew in sculpted arrangements of arrows and circles across a silver blue sky.

On her fortnightly day off, Wilma had walked the ten miles home to the cottage in Diddington. Only her mother was living there still, and her next brother up, Nick, who worked as a farm labourer, and hadn't married, due, they all said, to being 'not quite right in the head'. Wilma supposed that if Nick had been alive today he wouldn't have been let off with such a vague diagnosis. He would have been handed a more precise or politically correct label, such as low IQ or intellectually challenged. But the outcome for him would have been exactly the same. He'd been well off, living in Diddington, where he was accepted for who he was, and paid £5 a week for his labours on Tom Quinn's farm, and housed with his mother, who worried about what would happen to Nick when she was dead. She needn't have worried, though, for Nick was killed by a new piece of farm machinery just before war broke out in 1939.

During the war, Wilma had gone with a friend into the

bright lights of Leicester. They'd both taken jobs in a munitions factory, and a bedsit behind the station. It was then that she met Larry. He was home on leave and had come into Leicester with a couple of mates to a Saturday night dance. Wilma and Dolly had worn identical dresses, one in blue and one in red, that they'd bought with their week's wages in the High Street. Fripperies, Evie would have called them. Larry had walked her home that evening, and his friend Ned had taken Dolly. Within three months both couples were engaged. Wilma had taken Larry home to meet Evie, who'd made a huge steak and kidney pudding with tender young runners from the garden and a late crop of new potatoes, and her own rhubarb and blackberry crumble to follow. Evie and Larry had been two of a kind: both with a calm strength running through them. Evie had worried almost as much as Wilma when Larry was reported missing, before he and Wilma had even had a chance to plan their wedding.

Wilma thought a lot about the past these days. Its figures – Evie, Larry, Dolly and Ned; Nick, and her other brothers and sisters, the Mellors, Tom Quinn – were more real to her in many ways than young Derrick's brood, and certainly more real than the others here in the Hotel Rhapsody Palas. The figures from the past had survived so much longer, they were simply more convincing. Moreover, so much of modern life seemed to Wilma so cheap and superficial: the computer games that Stevie and Simon played, staring for hour after hour at these little coloured symbols on a screen; the microwaves that made food so tasteless and the marriages that made a mockery out of wedding vows; schools that taught political fashions rather than what children needed to know to get on in life; hospitals that housed the latest dollar-rich technology rather than the healing benefits of loving care; television, with its repetition of the same programmes in different modes all the time – the soap operas, the quiz shows, the crime thrillers, the agony aunt programmes, in which people were made to bare the most unbelievable truths about their most private lives – even the news seemed to be made up to the same formula day after day.

The maid put a tray of tea on the table by Wilma's seat. She woke with a start; it wasn't quite the effortless return to consciousness practised by Lady Mellor at the Manor House all those years ago. 'Thank you, Bilge.' Wilma had made a point of learning the hotel staff's names and how to pronounce them. It came from having been in service herself. But she'd also found herself warming to the civility and sensitivity and *dignity* of these people, trying to make a living here on the southern shore of Turkey – where the land was reasonably fertile compared to the rest, but still nothing like as rich as the fields where Wilma lived – and where there were few other opportunities for jobs, apart from tourism. Take Bilge Hassoun, for instance: Wilma had found out through talking to Kizi Demir that Bilge was a farmer's daughter, with a husband who worked the land. They lived on the other side of the river. Every morning at six, Bilge rowed across; and every evening twelve hours later, back again.

That morning Bilge had spoken to Mehmet about the state of the Delancey girls' room, and he had spoken, man to man, to Crispin, who had spoken to Dodo, who had gone in there and shouted at them till they cleared it up. Bilge was always surprised that the English, who were supposed to be so civilized and cultured, could allow their children to behave like this.

On her way out of the hotel that evening, Bilge saw Martin

Holbeach hiring a car to take him to Dalaman. Apparently, he was flying back to London for a couple of days to sort out some business. She shook her head; there was *nothing* she understood about these English!

The old lady rowed her back. People were always surprised to find a grandmother doing the rowing. But the old lady's husband was long since dead, and her sons were away doing business in Marmaris. 'Allah didn't make me to be idle,' she always said. 'I'm happy as I am. I work for what I need, and when I've got it, I don't row any more. Sometimes the tourists, they come back from their little expeditions, and they don't find me here any more. I've skedaddled! And then they have to stand there and wave their arms until one of the boys sees them and brings a boat over. Of course, as soon as my sons have made their fortunes in Marmaris, they'll be back. Then they'll build me a fine little house to spend the rest of my days in, and they'll even buy me a television!'

By the pool in the Hotel Rhapsody Palas, Dodo and Grizelda were discussing education, about which Dodo was worried and Grizelda ought to know, being a professor.

'Jade's just done her GCSEs. We'll get the results when we get back. I don't think she's done very well – she was home only half an hour after the English exam started. She says it's eighty per cent continuous assessment, but I think she's only saying that to make me feel better. What do you think of the National Curriculum?'

Grizelda explained that she and Ronald had decided they were too concerned about the state of public education to expose Portia to it. 'She goes to a convent. You can count on nuns.'

'Our girls go to a comprehensive,' confessed Dodo. 'It isn't, of course, as most of the families where we live use the private sector.'

'Portia's got an extremely high IQ,' elaborated Grizelda. 'Ronald has a colleague in the psychology department who tested her. He said she needed to be somewhere where she felt safe and could develop one-to-one relationships with teachers.'

'Jade's teacher says she's never had such a bad relationship with anybody,' countered Dodo. 'She complains about her being insolent and unpunctual and untidy and generally just horrible. She says that if she doesn't improve she won't have her in her class any more.'

'Oh dear. Why don't you send her to a private school? There must be lots of them in Hampstead.'

'Oh we couldn't. We don't think it's right.'

'Oh.'

Perhaps it would be a good idea to be able to attach a figure to Jade and Star's intelligences, not that Dodo was in any real doubt about the quality of them. 'Of course, high IQ pupils ought to be treated as having special needs, just like those at the other end of the scale.'

'I thought that was the point I was making.'

'Was it?'

They move on to carpets, about which Dodo knew nothing, but Grizelda something, courtesy of her relationship with Ronald. 'I've been into a few of these shops,' said Dodo chattily, 'but I can't work out whether they're telling the truth or not. There was one I particularly liked, he said it was silk, and only fifteen million lire. Is that a lot?'

'It depends whether it was old or new, and where it came from.'

'I suppose you wouldn't consider coming to help me? I really would like to buy one for my sitting room.'

As there was no time like the present, especially on holiday, the two women set off for Karput, arranging to leave their children in the care of their fathers, whatever that meant.

The atmosphere in Karput was clammy, as though building up to a thunderstorm. Inside her tent dress, Grizelda perspired secretly, which was how she did most things. Dodo experienced a certain tightness round her chest, but whether that was due to the weather or the strains of being on holiday (the row with the girls that morning had been particularly unpleasant) she couldn't tell. They paused in front of several shops before selecting one to go in. It was run by a pair of brothers, who had a most un-Turkish looking blonde girl who spoke English with an American accent to act as translator. Soon the two women were seated cross-legged on the floor inside, which was a cool Aladdin's cave of rugs and carpets and prayer mats maintained at a pleasing temperature by a large white electric fan. Dodo explained what she wanted, and the young men displayed a number of possibilities. They asked if the ladies would like some apple tea. There was something wrong with the colouring of the carpets they'd been shown so far; Dodo knew what she wanted but she hadn't seen it yet. Grizelda was patiently trying to uncover the exact nature of the carpet in Dodo's mind. They drank the apple tea. As the prices of the carpets they'd been looking at were all in the £500–1500 range, the young men hoped that serious business would eventually be done, and so, as it was growing late, they offered the ladies a snack and a glass of Turkish white wine. 'Why not?' said Dodo. It had been a long time since lunch. She felt almost gay, released from the confines of her family.

The little meatballs tasted delicious. 'Home-made,' said the girl, beaming at them, though actually she'd nipped out the back of the shop and got them from the café down the road. The meatballs were chewed, and the wine flowed. Dodo's choice was narrowed down to two: 'What do you think?' She turned to Grizelda.

'Why not buy them both?' said Grizelda bountifully – it wasn't her money, after all.

Dodo's mood expanded. The blue and orange one would go well in the sitting room, and the one with green in it would look lovely in what she called her office, where she worked on the designs for her pottery. Didn't she deserve a treat? When had she ever spent much money on herself?

'I'll take them both,' she said quickly, before the decision slipped away from her, like many other golden opportunities in her life. She offered her Visa card (on the marital account) and made arrangements for the carpets to be parcelled up and delivered to south Hampstead.

'My God, what am I going to say to Crispin? I never would have had the courage without you!' she confessed to Grizelda as they made their way, slightly drunk, back to the hotel.

There was a board up in hotel reception: 'Don't forget Saturday night 8 p.m. Proper Holidays invites all its clients to a special poolside barbecue with champagne. Tickets available at reception.'

'That'll be nice,' muttered Grizelda, tripping over the hotel cat.

It was, except that Grizelda and Dodo proved to have disqualified themselves, not by buying too many carpets, but because of the meatballs.

'Forty per cent of tourists get the runs,' said Carly Atkins at the barbecue. 'You know what they say, "Travel broadens the mind and loosens the bowels." Have you got some kaolin?'

Her own throat was better, cured by a night with the owner of the Dircan restaurant – in fact the same night as the Delanceys' family quarrel.

'We must hope that it isn't something worse,' remarked Ronald Dunkerley precisely. 'Dysentery, for instance, or giardiasis.'

'Giardy-what?'

'A parasitic infection found in places where hygiene is poor. Like carpet shops.'

'Carpet-buying is a cause of marital discord in at least seventy per cent of our clients,' quoted Carly. She giggled. They weren't supposed to drink on duty.

'Is that seventy per cent of your married clients, or seventy per cent of all your clients, in which case what percentage are married?' inquired Ronald pedantically. Happily he was distracted by a view of Sandy Holbeach in a shoulderless apricot pink dress. She looked fairly dashing, with her dark hair piled in a snake's coil on top of her head.

'We're a bit depleted tonight, aren't we?' he commented to her, looking around. The Welsh bird-watchers were away on a trip. There had been reports of a sighting of the marbled teal north of Punka. Beverley Myers, the honeymooner, and her new husband were planning the bedroom in their Essex starter home while watching the sunset from a boat in the middle of Lake Dinya.

'An upholstered headboard with built-in dimmer switches,' Bev murmured.

'My suits next to your dresses in a walk-in cupboard,' responded he.

'Don't start me off again,' pleaded Sandy to Ronald. 'I've

only just got myself together.' The rumours of a sniffle started at the back of her nose.

'What was the problem? The Bosnian crisis, was it? Sometimes world events catch up with one.' Seeing Sandy's expression, he hastily added, 'Oh, I'm not defending your husband's behaviour. *I* wouldn't have gone home for a similar crisis at the university. Not that there's much going on there at this time of year.' He thought mournfully for a moment about the current state of the universities – the threat of redundancies, the huge pressure to take more and more dim students and charge them increasingly extortionate fees for something which only those with liberal imaginations could call education. 'Ah, here we are!'

Bilge Hassoun was coming round with a tray of Turkish champagne. She was getting overtime. Her husband was none too pleased, but she'd promised to go into Ocakkoy on her day off next week and look at some new farm machinery with him.

'How is Grizelda?'

'Very weak. She's having some soup in bed. Portia is with her. She's a good girl, Portia.'

'Unlike my Josh, you mean,' responded Sandy self-punitively.

'No, I didn't mean that.'

'What did you mean then?'

'I only meant Portia isn't giving us any trouble. Yet.'

'No. Well.'

Ronald didn't seem to be saying the right thing. Which was a pity, as he really liked Sandy.

By the bar Crispin was having better luck with Meg Shaw. 'I've spent two days looking for you,' he complained. 'Why have you been avoiding me?'

'I don't want any complications.'

She was wearing that white dress again.

'Stuff that,' he urged. 'Don't you want to *live*?'

She laughed. 'I *am* living.'

'Come away with me tonight. We'll hire a boat and go up to the lake and swim by moonlight, and then after that . . .'

'Yes I know, you'll take me off into the reeds and make love to me while your poor wife is lying prostrate in her room.'

'You don't take me seriously.'

'You don't take yourself seriously.'

'You're right, of course.' Her observation recalled to Crispin the underlying unease he felt at being who he was, the way he was. He turned away towards those serious reminders of death, the rock tombs, which were now in shadow on the face of a mountain black against a deepening but still sun-streaked sky.

Round the pool the lights were lit, and Kizi was getting the barbecue going. Two of the hotel cooks were coming out with trays laden with meat and vegetables. Mehmet had slotted a tape of classical favourites into the hotel's loudspeaker system, and Pavarotti was singing 'Nessun Dorma'. 'Oh, I do like his voice,' said Lisa Upton, swooningly, 'it's so *masculine*!'

'Yukky music,' remarked Jade to Joshua and Aaron who were, unusually, sitting in more or less the same place. 'And we can't even watch telly. Whoever heard of a four-star hotel without television? We're missing *EastEnders*, and *Casualty* and *Neighbours*. Are we really going to spend the evening here with the oldies?'

'Why don't we wait a bit till they're properly settled in, and then make off somewhere?' suggested Kelly.

'We could take some of the food and some drinks and go to the beach.'

'How would we get there?'

'I'm sure we could find a boat to take us.'

'It's illegal after dark.'

'A lot of things are illegal in Turkey. Doesn't mean they don't happen.' Joshua had a new consignment of hash-hash in his pocket.

The coals of the barbecue heated up and the smell of charred flesh mixed with that of the bougainvillaea and the women's perfumes. 'It makes me feel sick,' confided Star to Aaron. 'It's quite unnecessary to eat animal flesh, don't you think?'

'Not to mention the environmental pollution,' observed Aaron, sniffing.

'If we go to the beach we mustn't disturb the baby turtles.' Star was torn by conflicting motives: excitement and adventure, on the one hand, and environmental concern, on the other.

'Fuck the turtles,' retorted Joshua. 'The earth's a cruel place. And it belongs to us.'

'You mean us particularly?'

'I mean us particularly.'

Star looked up. The half moon that was there seemed incredibly bright. But then the air was clearer here than in south Hampstead; the moon's light had less to contend with trying to make its imprint on the earth.

'Are you coming, Aaron?' Star sensed a kindness and a stability in him that was missing in Joshua Holbeach. Her own temperament and her role as Jade's shadow led her to be cautious.

'Might as well.' Aaron, too, was bored by the proceedings tonight. He'd rather have been at home in W6 with his mates, or reading books about the new techniques of chronometric dating, including amino-acid racemization and thermoluminescence. If his mother hadn't been so obviously otherwise engaged, he'd have suggested a moonlit trip to the ruins the other side of the river, which they'd not yet visited. But he could see from here that all her attention was being taken by Star and Jade's father. On the whole, Aaron took a philosophical view of his mother's relations with men. When he'd been younger, he'd felt threatened, but now he'd learnt that the men came and went. One of them might be the flavour of the month for a while, but they never lasted. Meg said she wasn't very good at living with them and there was always a point at which living together came up. Aaron could see what she meant. His mother had some pretty unsavoury habits, like taking all her paperwork and many of her meals to bed. She'd got a little portable television by the bed and a two-bar electric fire and a succession of very expensive boxes of chocolate Bath Oliver biscuits. She got up a nice chocolate-y fug. And then there was her housekeeping style – or rather the lack of it. That was why they didn't seem to have any of the normal 'why-don't-you-clear-up-your-room' sorts of rows other parents and teenagers had. Sometimes Meg would say to him despairingly (standing in the living room or the kitchen), 'We've got to do something about this place, Aaron!' And then the two of them would put their gas masks on and get the black plastic sacks out and grapple with the ancient Hoover (a leaving present from one of the men) and reward themselves with a take-away crispy duck and pancakes.

Aaron's friends envied him his laissez-faire mother. Sometimes he envied them their live-in fathers. But whenever he got close, he saw the down side: the rows, the competition, the marriages about to break up, or just held together because-of-the-children. At least I'm no excuse for anything, he told himself. And then there were the social work stories his mother brought back: abandoned home-alone children, seriously hit women, blokes who squandered the dole on beer and never had anything that hadn't come off the back of a lorry, women who did the streets to feed their kids – it made your heart bleed for the human race, except that race was racist and his mother's social work department was good on equal opportunities, as it was cheaper to clean up your language than anything else.

'Come on, let's get some food organized.'

Star and Aaron, Joshua and Jade, Kelly and Simon piled their plates and took a heap of paper napkins, and Jade went round to Kizi and whispered something in his ear about doggie bags. At first Kizi didn't understand (not many Americans came here) but then he went off to the kitchen and came back with some heavy-duty paper bags.

Portia Holbeach, in attendance on her sick mother, saw all this provisioning going on from the window of her mother's room. 'I'm hungry, Mum,' she said. 'Can I go and get something to eat?'

'Of course, darling, I'll be all right for a bit.' Grizelda felt as though an army had been sitting on her stomach. She was full of kaolin, which made her feel even heavier, and had just taken some codeine for her headache, which would succeed in bunging her up even further.

'What are you doing?' hissed Portia to Jade.

'Be quiet! We're going on a little expedition.'

'Can I come?'

Jade looked at her witheringly.

'We did promise,' Star reminded her, thinking of the glasses.

'Oh well, I guess so.'

'We can't all leave at once,' said Joshua, 'they'll get suspicious. I'll go first. The rest of you should leave at five minute intervals. We'll meet down by the harbour. I'll go and hassle for a boat.'

Thirty minutes later a boat that could have been a fishing vessel, but wasn't, silently passed the bright lights and animal smells of the Hotel Rhapsody Palas. Sitting at a table close to the river's edge, Crispin and Meg saw the boat, but thought nothing of it. The other side of the pool, sitting sideways on two sunbeds gnawing their way through thick lamb kebabs, Ronald and Sandy licked meat juices off their fingers without a thought for their own parental responsibilities. Derrick Upton was entertaining Lisa and the honeymooners to an imitation of John Major; Lisa had seen it before, but she enjoyed other people thinking Derrick funny. Also, Derrick had told her before they left their room that evening that he'd been doing some sums and they'd be able to afford both his nose job and her sky blue runaround after all. Nothing made Lisa happier than the prospect of spending money.

Joshua had persuaded the Karput boat co-operative to let him pilot the boat himself. The money that he'd taken from his father's wallet helped. Josh had learnt boating at his school. He was good at lots of things, but particularly those involving some manual or physical skill. What he'd really like to be was a master craftsman making fine objects out of wood.

'D'you think he knows what he's doing?' whispered Star to Jade.

'Of course he does, silly.' She admired the masterful way Joshua was standing there moving the – what was it called? The tiller. She couldn't imagine her father behaving like that – taking control, working out what to do and then doing it.

At first Joshua stuck fairly closely to the river bank where there were lights, so he could see what he was doing. Then, when they went round the corner and Karput and the hotel disappeared from view, he switched on the battery-operated lights on the mast of the boat.

'This is great, isn't it!' said Simon Upton, a little nervously.

'When can we eat?' Portia was still starving, and when she was hungry that was all she could think about.

'When we get there.' Fortunately it wasn't difficult to get to the sea. There were no wrong turns to be made; only the tracks of the dark reed-spattered water to be followed. It was cool out here in the river; the night air was mixed with a fierce salty breeze. Joshua dragged his pullover from the bottom of the boat.

'What was that?' Kelly was startled, her eyes rounded, by a harsh sound from the reeds.

'Probably a marsh frog or a terrapin. Nature's a noisy thing.'

Jade went to stand next to Joshua at the helm. He put his arm round her. The boat swerved. 'Watch what you're doing!' rebuked Kelly sharply. 'Cut the lovey-dovey stuff, for God's sake!'

When they reached the mooring platform by Turtle Beach, Simon jumped out with the rope. They tied up the boat and took their bags of food. The beach was dark and empty of everything except for the outlines of chairs and tables and folded umbrellas, which picked up what moon- and starlight there was. Far away, it seemed, the sea, rippled with patches of etiolated light, advanced and receded with a gentle lunar pulse. Joshua turned on a torch. 'Put that off,' instructed Star sharply.

'Aw, come on.'

'I mean it. There's enough moonlight to see by.'

'For us, or for the fucking turtles?'

'Both.'

Joshua dropped the torch in the boat. It wasn't worth fighting over.

'It's cold.' Portia shivered.

'Here, have my jacket.' Aaron handed it over, and added, to cheer her up, 'You never know, we might turn up your glasses!'

They took the food down nearly to the water's edge and sat down in the damp sand. Jade handed it out. It was hard to see in the semi-light. Star got a piece of meat by mistake and flung it in the ocean in disgust.

'Hey, that's good nutrition! There are people in the Third World who'd be glad of that.'

'This is the Third World,' she pointed out.

'Okay, okay. We don't want no political lectures now.' Joshua bent forward so the juice from his kebab dripped on to the sand. Kelly opened a can of Pepsi. 'We can do better than that.' He took two half bottles of vodka out of his pocket.

'Where d'you get those?'

'Dosh. Dosh reaches things nothing else does.'

Jade unscrewed the first bottle and tipped it to her lips. The bottle caught the light, which was reflected back on the whiteness of her face and neck against her black hair; the black sky, the cavernous ebony ocean. Joshua ripped the bottle from her, laughing. 'Two can play at that game!' He fell on top of her; they tumbled and twisted in the sand. The others turned away. Aaron looked apprehensively at the sky, where clouds were blotting out the light of the stars. They'd left a light on the boat running, so they could find it again. He wondered how long the batteries would last.

Joshua stood up. 'Who's for a swim, then?'

'We haven't brought our bathers.'

'Who cares?' He stripped down to his Calvin Klein underpants. Everyone looked away except Jade. 'Come on, Jade, come in with me.' He slipped an arm round her waist, began to wrestle with her t-shirt.

'I don't think you should, Jade,' protested Star. 'You've only just eaten. You know Mum says we shouldn't swim straight after eating.'

'Mummy's girls are we?' mocked Joshua. Jade lifted the vodka bottle to her lips again. Joshua pulled her shorts down. She stood there on the beach in bra and pants. Joshua began to kiss her. She threw her white neck back.

'Stop it!' shrieked Portia suddenly. 'We don't want a sex show!'

Joshua turned to her and laughed. He took Jade's hand and together they walked into the sea.

'You don't want to swim, do you?' Aaron asked Star.

She shook her head, looking, he thought, rather desolate. 'I think I'll go in with them, just to keep an eye on things.'

She nodded. 'Thanks, Aaron.'

It was by now quite clear that something was happening in the sky: the clouds were slowly but surely organizing themselves into a storm. It had been threatening for days, with weather which even for southern Turkey had been oppressively hot. The revellers back at the Hotel Rhapsody Palas's Proper Holidays barbecue noticed it. Kizi pointed: 'The Gods will be angry tonight.'

'"Angels mumbling", my mother called it.' Meg Shaw took two glasses of wine back to the table by the river. She gave one to Crispin. He held it up, as though inspecting it for imperfections.

'I love you,' he said, hardly looking at her.

'Nonsense,' she replied, in her best social worker voice.

'I do, I do,' he moaned. 'I can't get you out of my head. Ever since the first day of the holiday, when I saw you diving into the pool in your golden —'

'— yellow M and S,' she interrupted.

'Shut up, bikini. I've been obsessed by you since then.'

She sits back in her chair, laughing. 'Crispin, you're a married man here on holiday with your wife and two daughters. Your life is with them.'

'You don't understand,' he pleaded, reaching for her hand in the thundery darkness. 'I've not felt like this since I was a teenager. I feel alive. Life is full of hopes and meaning. I want you, Meg! I want to be a part of you. I want to be joined to you. I want to join my life to yours. I want to make love to you in the moonlight, in the starlight, in the sunlight, in the everything light.'

Above them, the first rumble of thunder is heard.

'Looks like the evening's coming to a premature end,' remarked Ronald Dunkerley to Sandy Holbeach. They had migrated to a more comfortable seat to the right of the barbecue, overlooking the pathway into Karput, and the place where the local river-crossing boats were moored.

'I'd better go and check on the children,' said Sandy.

Ronald nodded. He admired responsible motherhood in a woman. 'Can I get you anything while you're gone? More coffee? Wine? A cognac, perhaps?'

'That would be nice.' She smiled at him, and a strand of her glossy hair escaped its confines on top of her head and fell over her shoulders, covering her seashell ear, but revealing her vulnerability anew. It occurred to Ronald that he'd like to see all of her with all her hair down.

Kizi and the other staff were beginning to clear up the barbe-cue. Bilge and Suleyman were taking the umbrellas down and removing the mattresses from the sunbeds to protect them from the rain. The music pouring from the loudspeakers changed to Gershwin's 'Rhapsody in Blue'. 'Dum der dum,' sang Ronald, drumming on the table with his fingers. He got up to order the cognacs. The other side of the bar, Crispin Delancey was holding Meg Shaw's hands between his own in a gesture that looked very much like pleading. Ronald felt momentary guilt about Crispin's wife and his own confined to their beds by the gastro-intestinal side-effects of carpet-buying. He slipped over to the other side of the pool and opened the door to the Dunkerley room very quietly. Grizelda was asleep. Portia wasn't there, but Ronald was sure he'd seen her somewhere about recently, eating. So that was all right, then.

Another rumble of thunder, and another. But it was a long way away still. Maybe it was something electric in the atmos-phere, but Professor Ronald Dunkerley couldn't bear to think of the evening ending just yet. Why, it had only just begun. Here he was, sitting with an attractive young(ish) woman, for the first time in God knows how long, on his own, in a highly romantic setting, and what was he going to do about it?

'Would you like to go for a midnight swim?' Ronald asked Sandy, as they sipped their cognacs.

She almost choked on hers. 'Where? What, in this weather?'

'We could take that boat' – he pointed to the nearest of the hotel rowing boats – 'and go across the river, and swim from there. The river's quite clean.'

'Are you sure?'

'Oh yes.' He smiled kindly at her in a manner not unlike the one he used for explaining to the college accountant that not everything in academic life could be measured in terms of money.

Back on Turtle Beach, the youth club was also responding to the electric current in the air. Jade and Joshua were behaving like badly tutored porpoises in the waves, and Aaron was admonishing them with threats of being struck by lightning. Portia and Star had cleared up the food. Simon was digging in the sand evilly looking for turtles' eggs, and Kelly was working out how she could get her own back on Jade Delancey for stealing Joshua Holbeach from her.

A not-so-distant rumble of thunder is followed by the first flash of lightning, zigzagging in mercurial brilliance across the surface of the navy blue sea. Jade was startled. 'What was that?' Her hair was joined seamlessly to the waves.

'That was a warning from on high,' said Aaron. 'Telling you it's time to get out. Please. There's going to be a real storm, and we've got to get these kids back to the hotel. If you two aren't coming, we'll go without you.'

'You won't be able to manage the boat.'

'You do learn some things at state schools, Josh.' Aaron didn't say this unkindly, but it was enough to get Joshua out of the sea.

There was another flash of lightning while Jade and Joshua and Aaron turned their backs and struggled out of their wet underclothes and back into shorts and t-shirts. The lightning made the white flesh of their backs gleam like swordfish. Everyone else was waiting on the boat. Portia was shivering and even Kelly seemed a little frightened. Josh looked at all of them. 'Don't be scared, kids, it'll be all right. Uncle Josh'll get you home. In only a few minutes you'll all be back with your mummies and daddies!'

They cast off, and Joshua started the motor. It didn't catch at first, which caused a good deal of breathholding. Then it did, and they were away. Out in the middle of the dark river with only the reeds and hidden birdlife for company, the lightning came again, dashing across the sky and into the earth followed by thunder that felt as though it was going to split the boat . . .

Portia sat very close to Kelly and Simon, who were abnormally silent. And then the rain started. It was as though everything was inverted, and the river was falling out of the sky. Although Joshua rolled the sailcloth across the top of them, it was intended to cut out the sun, not this kind of liquid beating, which lashed out at everything. 'It's exciting really,' said Simon, looking up at the embattled sky.

'Do you think they'll miss us?' asked Portia hopefully.

'Na. Shouldn't think so.'

They probably wouldn't have done, had an unfortunate collision not occurred between the *Fidan* and the *Tuna I*, the Hotel Rhapsody Palas's number one rowing boat, which was just coming back from the opposite shore bringing the wet figures of Ronald Dunkerley and Sandy Holbeach, who were caught with their pants down in the river when the storm started. Joshua didn't see the smaller boat in time to stop, and Ronald, who was rowing, didn't have enough room to reroute the *Tuna I*, even when he had seen the larger boat advancing. 'Oh my God!' Sandy covered her face in the skirt of her wet apricot dress, and Ronald's mouth dropped open when he saw who was aboard the *Fidan*, particularly the pale figure of his good daughter, Portia.

SIX

Freedom and Desire

Crispin and Meg were in bed in Meg's room. Lightning flashed the carpeted concrete platform of the bed blue-white, and the pickled skeletons of the tubed fluorescent lights, and streaked the white cotton sheets where man and woman tangled, touching and thrashing, but not yet joining. 'Oh, you are wonderful,' cried Crispin, trying to undo Meg's bra. 'Are you sure you're really human? Maybe you're a goddess sent to taunt me.'

'Here, let me help.'

Her breasts fell out, and the lightning came again, turning them into little silver moons, upon which Crispin's mouth must predictably fall. His hands moved down. Meg's waist was much thinner than Dodo's, her pubic hair softer. The insides of her thighs were pure silk. He wanted to be down there too, licking, tasting, eating, losing himself in her. For some reason Woody Allen's remark in *Crimes and Misdemeanours* came back to him: 'The last time I was inside a woman was the Statue of Liberty.' Meg Shaw was Crispin's Statue of Liberty: his path to freedom, away from the constraints of marriage and fatherhood and everything else he thought he'd chosen, but hadn't really.

When he took his pants off, helped, it had to be said, by her, his penis leapt out into the darkness like the rod he remembered from his youth. She took it in her white hands and then her pink mouth and it was all he could do to prevent himself losing himself in her there and then.

'Have you got a condom?' she whispered.

'What? No, of course not.'

'I have. Wait a minute.'

She handed him a packet. He looked at it distastefully. His penis drooped.

'Don't worry, I'll put it on for you.'

'But I don't want to use a bloody condom, I want to feel you.' He felt masterful. He got on top of her and pinned her hands down on the bed. He moved from mouth to nipple and back again; she was aroused, her breaths were shallow, her neck was flushed, and when he put his hand between her legs a tributary of the river Dinacek was flowing there.

He slid himself condom-less into her, and held himself there, stiff and full. She moaned and turned her head from side to side. 'You like that, don't you, Mrs Goddess?' His smile, framed by whitened curls, was gentle and loving, and her closed eyes opened suddenly like periwinkles on a Swiss mountain. 'I love you, Meg,' he sighed, beginning to move slowly. 'I love you, I love you, oh . . .' His final shudder was sharp and quick like the lightning which shot into the room just as Aaron opened the door.

He stood there for a moment, wet from his boating trip. 'You should lock the door next time,' he said.

Round the other side of the hotel about twenty minutes later Dodo Delancey woke up to the sound of Crispin having a shower.

'What on earth are you doing having a shower in the middle of the night? Are the girls all right?' she asked sleepily.

'Of course.' Crispin had briefly encountered his daughters

after he left Meg's room. They'd both been wet through – they said they'd been into Karput for a walk.

Three rooms further down, the professors Dunkerley were having their own problems, as Ronald was finding it hard to come up with a satisfactory explanation for his own wetness, and the fact that his underpants had relocated to his trouser pocket. The best he could do was to argue that, under the influence of the party and the approaching storm, a whole group of them had decided to take a dip in the swimming pool, but as it was late, they hadn't wanted to disturb their various spouses and children by rummaging through rooms looking for swimming costumes. It was a version of events that acquired conviction as he told it, but rapidly lost that when Grizelda informed him that she'd peeked out of her door at about the same time the whole group was supposed to be skinny-dipping and the swimming pool had been quite empty: still as the sky on a cloudless day, in fact.

Portia was the other reason why Ronald realized he'd have to make a clean breast of it. What Portia had been doing on the other boat was as far beyond Ronald's comprehension as his presence on *Tuna I* with Sandy Holbeach was beyond hers.

What was he to do? Ronald stood in the doorway of their room cleaning his half-moon glasses. It was a distraction technique he used when he'd forgotten his lecture notes, or a particularly clever student (rarer and rarer these days) caught him out. There had been one shortly before he'd left on holiday who'd asked him, apropos of his third-year lecture on Church and State in the Ottoman Empire, how his casual remarks about the negligible role of women could be squared with the activities of 'A'isha, the prophet's widowed wife, who in AD 656 led an army at Basra in what became known as the Battle of the Camel, successfully inciting the population to sedition and civil war.

Grizelda was firing questions at him rather like Fatima, his questioning student.

Grizelda had come to marriage and motherhood late, only after sorting out her career first. When other girls had been interested in boys and the prevailing whims of teenage culture (in the 1960s in Bath where Grizelda had grown up), Grizelda had stuck to her books. Her particular passion for eighteenth-century writing – the century when the novel was born – had been generated by the chance find in a bookshop of a copy of Gardner's version of *The Book of Margery Kempe*. Grizelda had become a professor at the age of thirty-two, having published her thesis on *The Sacred and the Vernacular in Early English Writing*.

One reason for the success of Grizelda's work was that wrapped up in it was all the eroticism of mind and body that went unused in her life. The work sparkled with a sensual savagery that drew the reader in and on. Men fell in love with Grizelda's writing rather than with Grizelda. Meeting her was always a disappointment. So Ronald Dunkerley himself had felt when, having come across her book in an Athens bookshop while spending a summer with an archaeological friend at a minor dig north of Mycenae, he'd written to Grizelda enthusing about her work and suggesting a meeting to discuss a theme within it which was of particular interest to him – the intersection between militarism and religious ideology.

Although Grizelda's physical persona had been a disappointment to him, Ronald had known that one aspect he'd never tire of was her mind. On that basis, and because he himself was tired of being a bachelor, he'd proposed marriage. He hadn't envisaged parenthood as well; marriage would have been quite enough for him. But Portia had been an easy, self-absorbed child, which was a mercy, because her parents had continued to be just as absorbed in their own work after she was born as they had been before. In fact, when Portia was four weeks old, Grizelda had wheeled the pram to Boots to buy some nursery supplies, and had left it there for the rest of the day, going directly to the university library to resume her work on what was to become book number four. 'I forgot,' she'd said, when the police caught up with her. '"Like as the arrows in the hands of a giant even so are the young children,"' she'd quoted to them. 'It's part of the Churching of Women after childbirth service. Children make women unclean, you see. Charles Lamb used it in his "A Bachelor's Complaint" – one of the *Essays of Elia*, you know.'

Unlike Dodo Delancey, Grizelda Dunkerley did not see a happy marriage as essential to a satisfactory sense of self, and therefore as something to be pursued at all costs. But if she was to have a marriage, then it would have to be an unproblematic one: Ronald would not be allowed to wander from the straight and narrow.

'You weren't in the swimming pool, so where were you?'

'Grizelda, please!' Ronald didn't like raised voices, or arguments of any kind, except the intellectual. 'The river,' he said. Which, after all, was the truth.

'Why didn't you say that to begin with?'

'I knew you'd complain about the dirty water.'

'I would, if you dragged Portia into it, or I went in it. Especially after whatever it was they gave us in that carpet shop.' She clutched her stomach, which was still laced with pains. 'What I find particularly awful,' she went on, 'is that you were out enjoying yourself while I was lying here ill. And I don't know where Portia was, either. She was out there eating when I went to sleep. Where did she go after that?'

'I don't know.'

In the morning, Portia was waiting for him in the garden. 'Hallo, Daddy!'

She suddenly looked rather like her mother. 'Did you tell Mummy where you were last night?'

'No. Did you tell her where you were?'

'Well, no.'

'That's two of us, then, isn't it?' There seemed no answer to this. 'What *were* you doing, Daddy?'

'I went for a boat ride with Mrs Holbeach.'

'Where was Mr Holbeach?'

'He's gone back to London for a few days.'

'So you were keeping Mrs Holbeach company?'

'That's right.' It struck Ronald that he should be interrogating Portia, rather than the other way around.

'If you're going to ask me where I was,' said Portia determinedly, 'I was keeping Jade and Star and Joshua and Aaron and Kelly and Simon company.'

'Ah.'

'We're having a good holiday, aren't we, Daddy?' She skipped off into the undergrowth like a spring lamb.

Ronald sat down to think. Things seemed to be getting out of control. It wasn't what he'd expected when Perkins in the history department had recommended the Karput package from Proper Holidays. He didn't like the effect on Portia of associating with these other youngsters. The Uptons were – well, not the kind of people they'd usually associate with. Ronald had had so little to do with people from social classes other than his own, that he wasn't even aware that he despised them. The Delanceys and Martin Holbeach seemed a bit left-wing. He had no impression of Sandy's politics, but he sensed – correctly – that they'd probably be rather liberal, that is, malleable.

He didn't understand what had come over him with Sandy yesterday. It must be something in the air. Holidays were bad for you. He must take a grip on himself.

He bent down and strapped up his Clarks sandals more tightly. As he stood up grip-like, a group of bird-watchers advanced towards him. One of them, white-haired, red-faced and lean, not unlike a stork, held out a claw-like hand. 'Dai Evans.'

'Ronald Dunkerley.'

'We've just come from Karput. On our way back from Punka, you know: we saw a lemon-breasted black-headed bunting. The point is, we saw something in Karput we thought one of you ought to know about.'

'One of who?'

'Put it this way. A dark lad, about sixteen or seventeen. Smokes. We don't know who he belongs to, but we've seen the young people congregating together.'

'Whom,' corrected Ronald, automatically. 'That would be Joshua Holbeach.'

'It would? Not yours, then?'

'Nothing to do with me,' said Ronald firmly.

'Well, he's up to no good, you can take it from us. Drug-dealing, we'd say, wouldn't we?' Dai turned round to the group behind him, who all nodded in assent like a group of co-nesting warblers. 'You can get done for drug-dealing in Turkey. They take a much stiffer view than the authorities back home. We thought you ought to know.'

'Well, thanks very much. I'll pass the message on.'

'Our pleasure.' Dai and his gang turned like an army on a command, and with a chorus of clicks from their binoculars moved away.

Ronald walked down to the riverside where Portia and Simon Upton were throwing things into the water. 'Listen to me, Portia. I want you to stay away from Joshua Holbeach in future, do you hear me?'

Portia looked round wide-eyed. 'Why, Daddy? Does that mean you're going to stay away from Mrs Holbeach?'

'Don't talk to me like that, Portia!'

He went inside and sat down in the hotel reception. At least it was cool: a white fan was blowing over the blue- and white-tiled floor. Mrs Blake was in there reading the *Daily Mail*.

'Look at this, Professor Dunkerley,' she said, showing him the front page: 'Andrew: I'll Stand By You' it said, over a picture of Fergie in a pink-flowered dress with her financial adviser. 'What do you think?' asked Mrs Blake eagerly. 'Are they guilty or not?'

'Is nothing sacred?' said Ronald to himself.

'I beg your pardon?'

'What's happening to us, Mrs Blake?' asked Ronald wearily.

Wilma looked at him quizzically. She seemed to be about to say one thing, and then she said another. 'Well, I don't know about you, but I'm finding it a bit hot. And the *Mail* gets here a day late. I might ring up one of my friends in Diddington – maybe these photos they keep mentioning are published by now.' She smiled and did one of her minor witch-like laughs.

Ronald didn't say anything, so Wilma Blake went on. 'I don't see why the royal family should be different from the rest of us. I mean they are, aren't they, due to being royal, but there's no reason why they shouldn't have the same problems. Take Fergie now, she's a free-spirited young woman, it doesn't take an expert to see that she's not going to take kindly to being told to toe the line. And them young princes – well, Charlie's hardly young any more, is he – they're not used to being told what to do, neither. I dare say the Queen's done her best to be a good mother, but there's no guidebooks on how to bring up a king, is there?'

Ronald had the distinct impression that she was leading him on and didn't believe any of this. As she spoke, he also began to feel he'd met her somewhere before. Behind the little old lady demeanour there lurked another persona, a different past.

The point about guidebooks was a good one, though. Maybe that was part of the problem – the lack of guidebooks for troubled parents trying to bring up teenagers. Ronald had only the vaguest notions about the youth drug scene. His strongest feeling was the same as yesterday – pity for Sandy Holbeach. He sighed. He'd better tell her.

'Come in.' Sandy was sitting in front of the mirror in her room applying Estée Lauder light-diffusing make-up. Behind her on the floor, Freddie was lying on his back with a police car balanced on his tummy, and Primrose was drawing a storm in her colouring book.

'I – er . . .' Ronald didn't know quite what to say. 'I mean, can we have a word?' On the floor by the dressing table he noticed two empty brandy bottles.

Freddie made a large brm-brm noise with his police car, and Primrose coloured furiously. 'When is Daddy coming back, Mummy?' asked Primrose in a loud voice.

'I've told you, darling, tomorrow or the next day. You can go swimming now if you want to,' she offered.

'We don't, do we, Freddie?'

Sandy looked up at Ronald despairingly.

'Perhaps if you could just come outside for a minute,' he suggested diplomatically.

She came out, all but shutting the door behind her. Pale pink roses on the trellis above her head diffused their brightness into her make-up. Ronald longed to touch her face, but a butterfly did so instead, flicking its vanilla wings lightly against its soft creamy contours.

'Look,' he began.

'If it's about last night, you don't need to apologize.'

'It isn't,' he said. There was a pause, during which the butterfly passed between them again. 'No, it's about Joshua, I'm afraid.' A look of alarm passed through her greyish eyes. 'No, nothing dreadful's happened. It's just that one of the bird-watchers said they'd seen him buying drugs in Karput.'

She sighed. 'I expect it's only hash. But he knows he shouldn't do it here. I'll speak to him later. He's not here now, I haven't seen him since last night. Thank you.' The look of pink happiness she'd had a moment ago was stripped from her face. She looked twenty years older, vanquished, worn down by responsibility.

'Is there anything I can do to help?' he asked.

'I wish there were. But I'm not sure there's anything *anyone* can do.' There might have been tears in her eyes as she shut the door.

An idea came to Ronald then. He would go and find Joshua and talk to him himself. After all, Joshua's father wasn't here, and according to Crispin Delancey didn't care much for the role of father anyway.

'I'm just going for a walk, dear,' said Ronald, putting his head round the door of their room. But Grizelda and Portia were nowhere to be seen. He left them a note: 'GONE FOR A WALK. BACK SOON.'

He strode manfully into Karput. The sun was high, and most of the tourists were in the sea, the river or the over-chlorinated swimming pools. Ronald peered into every bar he passed, looking for signs of Joshua Holbeach. Of course, the boy could be absolutely anywhere, but there was a good chance he'd be somewhere in Karput, especially if he were with a local drug gang. The only thing Ronald knew about drugs was that the word 'hash' came from the same root as the Turkish word 'assassin'. He vaguely assumed that, in order to have drugs, you had to have drug gangs, though how you recognized these he didn't know. He recalled a leaflet they'd had through their door recently from the council: 'What Every Parent Needs to Know about Drugs'. He hadn't read it, assuming he wasn't Every Parent, and so didn't need to know.

His peering got more feverish, but there was still no sign of Joshua. He went into every bar and tourist shop between the hotel and the harbour. Then he sat down on an orange bench outside a bank. In front of him were boards advertising boat trips: 'Thursday we make a trip to the lake of Dinya. Afterwards we got to Cesu, you can walk through the amberforest. After that we will drink tea by a farmer.' A young man came over towards him. 'You want boat trip? Very cheap, only hundred thousand lire.' Ronald shook his head. Perhaps that's where Joshua had gone. He looked upstream, where the sun formed a pool of gold and the river turned out of view. He looked downstream, where boats busied themselves moving tourists up and down to the sea, the wide, empty sea, which stretched from here all the way to the Greek islands, Crete, and the continent of Africa. Ronald thought back to that summer in Greece, when he'd met Grizelda's mind for the first time. No, it would be wrong to think of it as a mistake. Quite wrong.

He got up after a bit and moved on. There was a map of Karput at the other end of the harbour. A large red foxglove obscured it. Ronald moved it, but it sprang back like a jack-in-the-box. He walked the other way out of the village. There was another bar on the left-hand side. Peering was difficult, as it was very dark inside this one, but there did seem to be a group of youths in there. Ronald walked past again to see if he could spot Joshua, and then a third time to check that it really was him. The fourth time he intended to go in, but he realized he didn't quite know what he was going to say.

While he was debating how to go about his manly act, Joshua came out of the bar with three youths. They were laughing, and they walked along the road slapping each other's backs and generally behaving like friends. Joshua's black jeans had large holes at the knees, and his grey t-shirt had what looked like a large quantity of mud on it. Ronald followed them at a distance of a few metres. He fished in his trouser pocket for his clip-on sunglasses. When they passed a shop selling tourist clothes, on an impulse he nipped in and bought himself a green canvas hat. He tried to see himself in the window of a shop further down the street, but there was somebody the other side of the glass looking at him, so he could only hope for the best.

They all went along in this manner for half an hour or so, until they came out of Karput on the other side, where the road led through flat marshland, round a rocky peninsula and up and down a series of minor hills until it reached Turtle Beach. The convolutions of the road were the reason most people took a boat there. Ronald wondered where the gang was going. He tried to keep a good distance away, and as they left Karput behind, this meant darting in and out of the tall reeds and grasses that bordered the road and were no doubt home to the warblers and other wildlife Dai Evans and his troupe had come to see.

The boys stopped after a bit and lit cigarettes. They had to turn away from the slight wind that ran off the sea to light their matches, and Ronald had to swing abruptly into the reeds to avoid being seen. He fell over into a ditch and his new green hat fell off. He picked it up, and shook it to get the dust off. Something chirped at him from the smooth yellow stems of the reeds. Something else moved at ground level, something long and thin. He froze. It slithered past him. What was he doing crouching in these Turkish reeds with a water snake for company? Was this what he'd meant when he'd left a note for Grizelda and Portia: 'GONE FOR A WALK. BACK SOON.'? The four youths turned right, away from the road towards the river bank. The river here formed a calm inlet, like a lake. There was a platform jutting out in the middle of it, and a boat moored alongside. The four of them got in and rowed off. They rowed towards a little island in the middle, where a crop of swaying purple flowers suggested another conciliatory idea to Ronald: he would, on his way back through Karput, buy Grizelda some flowers. In fifteen years of marriage he'd never done that, supposing Grizelda not to be the sort of woman you gave flowers to, but he was just beginning to realize that even professors of history can make elementary mistakes; however, being professors of history, maybe they have a better chance of learning from them than other people?

They seemed to be looking for something on the island with the purple flowers. Ronald couldn't see what at this distance, and cursed himself for the second time that day, on this occasion for not being properly equipped like a bird-watcher. Whatever it was, they'd found it, and were rowing back. Ronald retreated into the reeds, more carefully this time. Four pairs of feet went past, all looking huge. Ronald felt particularly small crouched there in the marshes of Karput. He got out and followed them again. One of them was swinging some white powder in a plastic bag. He couldn't hear what they were saying. On the outskirts of the village, just before the first Pansiyon 'Everytime Hot Water' sign, Joshua turned round suddenly and walked back towards Ronald. 'Fucking shit, man,' he said, 'is this some kinda game or what? Why doncha go and play someplace else? You can leave off following my ma round too.'

Ronald was still thinking of what to say when Josh and his friends were a dust cloud in the distance. Weakly he trooped back into Karput in search of flowers. As he passed the bars, he peered into them as a matter of habit, including the one which Josh had come out of, and was surprised to see Derrick Upton sitting there instead, laughing and joking in a similar way with a group of dark Turkish men – though they were bound to look dark, given the absence of light inside, in contrast to the hot sun, from which Ronald's new hat, muddied from the reeds, was supposed to protect him.

SEVEN

Postcards Home

Wilma Blake was writing postcards in the rose garden. The scent of the flowers reminded her of her cottage garden back home. Her garden was nothing special: just the usual wild pink cottage ramblers, tall apricot foxgloves, red Jacob's ladder, blue cornflowers, yellow goldenrod and bunches of dark purple lavender. There was a vegetable patch which Wilma planted with lettuces and spring onions and new potatoes, and where lemon mint grew as though it owned the place, the yellow lines on its leaves cheekily annunciative of its right to be there.

Wilma had the postcards laid out in front of her: two of turtles, two of the rock tombs, two of Karput by night, and one of Caunos. The two night-time ones she'd send to her great-nieces in Leeds, who at fifteen and seventeen were more interested in night life than turtles or archaeological monuments. She printed their names carefully on the cards: 'SHELAGH' and 'ANNETTE DAWES'. The turtles would go to her friend Vera in the village and to Stan, who had a part-time job in a local wildlife park. 'Bet you can't match this!' she wrote, thinking of Stan in his neat cottage with everything just so, picking the card off the mat and chuckling at it and then putting it behind the square brown clock on the cream-tiled mantelpiece. The clock was electric – one of the first to be made, Stan had told her. The rock tombs were more difficult.

She should have bought more of the turtles. A wicked thought occurred to her. 'MRS BARBARA SCOTT' she printed with a smile on her face. 'How much do you think they paid to get buried up here?' she wrote, in the light of Barbara's unseemly preoccupation with the next life, and her long-running battle to secure a place for herself in the graveyard of Diddington church, though the vicar was unwilling to have her as they'd been full up since 1956, and Barbara only attended twice a year anyway. The last postcard went to a Ministry of Defence research station in Kent. 'Some people are better at defending themselves than others,' wrote Wilma. 'Will give you a ring when I get back. Time for the annual reunion soon!'

Wilma put the cards in her black handbag and clipped it shut. She'd take them to reception later, when she went to pick up yesterday's *Daily Mail*. She felt tired today, but she wasn't going to say anything to Derrick because he'd worry, which would make Lisa fuss in that irritating tinkly insincere way of hers. Wilma had tried hard to like Lisa, but Lisa used every opportunity to complain about other people in a holier-than-thou tone. It didn't suit her because you knew she wasn't. We've all got our particular vices, said Wilma to herself, think-ing of her own liking for solitude and gypsy creams and bacon with bread fried to a crisp unhealthy gold in its fat.

It was easy to see why Lisa found Wilma difficult – Derrick was an only son, and his father was only a memory. Wilma didn't feel she owned Derrick; the problem was that Lisa did. Wilma wasn't a bother to Derrick – she rang once a week, and took the train to Essex to see them two or three times a year, and every other time they'd come to her, and she'd make her raspberry sponge and coffee kisses and ham sandwiches with ham so thick and pink and freshly cut from Mr Cross's butcher's van that Kelly and Simon and Stevie thought it was a different breed of food from the ham they knew, which was square and pale and came shrink-wrapped from Tesco's. The children, now: Wilma would put up with any nonsense from any wife of Derrick's for the sake of the children. Little Stevie was her favourite: seven, and unspoilt, still thinking that she knew things he didn't. She could even forgive Simon his present rude behaviour, because he'd once been a Stevie. She could see the innocent child in him still, and beyond that the keen young man he'd one day become.

It was practice that gave you this way of looking at people so you could see their various selves layered there, like rings in the trunk of an oak tree. Time was the secret: time unlocked the difference between the good and the bad, the happy and the unhappy. Time took away some problems and gave you others. Time was on the side of the old, and not of the young. Mind you, it was more difficult with Kelly. Kelly had spirit. But Kelly was troubled. Wilma could see that Kelly alternated between aping her mother's curt, ambitious self-centredness, and her father's kinder and more democratic ways.

Wilma began to doze off in the shadowed fragrant place created by her parasol, the wooden seat and Suleyman's roses. She could have been sitting on the seat in her own garden, and it could have been one of her very own roses flavouring the air. There would be flowering borage at her feet, and next door's cat, a large white tom, would be sitting under the crab-apple tree. Wilma could just feel the village around her now, the village and the countryside in the full tide of summer. Along Cutting Lane the banks would be full of wild cornflowers and purple willowherb, and the baby pink flowers of the bindweed would sit like a child's plump toes amidst the dark gravel of the road. Pale golden grasses would wave along the edges of the fields, and the shorn sheep would have got used to being parted from their lambs, and the foal of the old horse Dusty would be stronger and taller than ever. Mrs Rowbotham would already be coming around collecting for the September Women's Institute jumble sale, and they would stand and chat by the pink and cream honeysuckle which draped the front frame of the cottage. The elderberries would be turning, ready for the wine that Stan was so good at making. The sky would be full of clear blue light all day, and there would be showers to give the flowers a drink, and settle the dust off everything. Perhaps that was what was wrong with this place: there was too much heat and dust. Rain came only in storms here, not in frequent renewing washings.

The seat shook a little, and Wilma opened her eyes: it would take more than a butterfly to create that kind of movement. Star Delancey had landed beside her: Star of the darkened hair and holey tights and impassive 'I don't really have any feelings' look.

'Are you all right, Mrs Blake?'

'Yes, dearie. Why?'

'Well, I just thought it's a bit early in the day to go to sleep.'

Wilma patted Star's black knee. 'I'm an old lady, dearie, we catnap a lot, you know, we drift off and think about the past.'

'Have you got an interesting past, Mrs Blake? You don't really want to be here either, do you?'

'Yes I have, dearie, and no I don't, not really. But it'll do. Sometimes there are things we must do for others, not for ourselves. I don't want my Derrick to feel guilty when I die. I don't want him to think, "Oh, I should have taken Mother on that holiday to Turkey," or "Oh, I should have gone to see Mother more often," or any such nonsense.'

'That's very generous of you.'

'It's not that you younger people don't have generosity in you,' said Wilma, understanding the nature of Star's comment, 'it's because you haven't learnt what to do with it yet.'

'I expect you're right.' Star removed a trailing line of mascara from under her right eye.

'It's not easy being young these days I don't expect,' went on Wilma encouragingly.

'I don't know, I've got nothing to compare it with. But I tell you this, Mrs Blake, I'm not sure we're in much more of a mess than our parents are.' Wilma agreed. 'Have you seen my dad and Aaron's mum together?'

'I have, dearie. And a few other things as well.'

'Me and my sister have just been in Karput. We went for a walk. Well, we went to have coffee with Yusuf and Celik – the two boys we met at the mud baths – but we didn't tell our parents that. The boys are really nice, you know. Mum thinks they're out to screw us' – Wilma flinched slightly at the language – 'but boys aren't like that in Turkey, they *respect* women. In fact, it's a lot safer here than at home. But try getting that over to Mum. She doesn't listen, she's got such fixed ideas. Anyway, I'm not into sex. It's too much to handle, what with AIDS and everything. And I think it's terribly overrated. What do you think, Mrs Blake?'

Wilma thought briefly about the past, when she had conjugated with men; Derrick's father, Bertram, until his lungs gave up, and then Charlie Blake, while his heart lasted, both in the cottage in Cutting Lane, though she had replaced the Silent Night in between. Bertram had been a big man and Charlie a little one, and the balance of the mattress had been decidedly different. Bertram had made love like he mixed the pigs' food or handled the combine harvester; there'd been a simple series of actions to perform, and that was it. He never talked about it. He never talked much about anything, anyway. But Charlie had been like a silky cat with her, licking her and playing with her everywhere, and paying her compliments, saying he could see moonshine in her hair, and that he only had to look in her lovely eyes and he was lost. She missed Charlie. Well, she missed Bertram, he was Derrick's father, but she missed the two men in different ways and for different things.

'But what were you saying, dearie?'

'Well, you know Mr Holbeach is supposed to have gone back to his office in England for a few days?'

'I was sitting in this very spot when he showed me the – what do you call it, that roll of paper thing –'

'A fax.'

'That's it, that the office had sent him.'

'Well, he hasn't gone. Jade and me saw him in Karput this morning.'

Wilma smiled to herself. 'Well I never! Now there's one for the books!'

'That isn't all, Mrs Blake.'

'It isn't?'

'He was dressed really oddly. He was wearing those baggy Turkish trousers and a long shirt, and he had a scarf over his head and face and he had some jewellery on and his eyes were . . .'

'Were what?'

Star clutched her stomach in a mixture of fear and hysteria.

'Well, made up, you know, with mascara and stuff, like mine. You see, Mr Holbeach was dressed up as a woman! We recognized him because of his bent shoulders. Joshua's got them, too.'

'Well I never!' said Wilma again. 'Mind you,' she said after a bit, 'that could fit.'

'Fit?'

'Yes, fit. Help to explain things. Oh, I don't mean why his son Joshua – he's basically a nice young man, you know, dearie, but I expect you do know that – why his son's behaving badly and why his wife's on the bottle.' Star's eyes widened. 'Yes, it takes a wise old woman like me to notice these things. It was on her breath the first day. But who wouldn't need a prop of some kind with a family like that to look after!'

'So what else does it explain?' pressed Star, moving closer on the seat with the unselfconscious urgency of a child.

'Oh, a few things. You'll see.'

'Tell me, Mrs Blake, tell me!'

'Patience, dearie. All things are unfolded in the fullness of time!'

Star sat for a few minutes treading the grass with her grainy scuffed black boots. 'These have got steel toecaps in them, you know,' she said inconsequentially.

'Well, if you like them I don't suppose they do anyone any harm.'

'What d'you think I should do about my dad and Aaron's mum?'

'What do you want to do, dearie?'

'I want them to stop!' Star sniffed, as though trying to contain tears.

'And you think you can make them do that?'

'Maybe.'

'Maybe you can. But remember, men of your father's age sometimes go through these phases.' She used the word advisedly as one she'd heard parents using about their children a lot these days. 'They go through these phases when the whole of their life flows before them and seems wasted, like a dried-up river. It makes them want to go back and do it all again. But they're frightened, so they have to find someone to go back with. Men are quite frightened creatures, really,' reflected Wilma, thinking about Mr Holbeach glimpsed in his feminine attire when he should have been manning the *Socialism Now* office. 'Anyway, dearie, the point is that most of them come to their senses given time. But maybe there's no harm in trying to speed the process up a little.' She cackled merrily.

'You do make me feel better, Mrs Blake. Why haven't I got a granny like you?'

'We don't choose our relations, dearie, only our friends, and we even get those wrong sometimes. But whatever you do, dear, do be careful. And now I must go and fetch my newspaper and get these postcards on their way.'

While Wilma Blake negotiated the price of stamps with Mehmet behind the reception desk, Ronald Dunkerley arrived back in the hotel looking for Grizelda and Portia. He wasn't sure he was any the wiser as a result of his youth-following trip, but he had said to Joshua, right there in the reedy marshes outside Karput, 'Now look here, I'm not following your mother around, and I'm only following you around for your own good. This – this business you're involved in is illegal. You could go to prison. Your mother is worried about you.' He realized after he'd said it that Joshua probably wouldn't be impressed that his mother was worrying about him. Joshua had given him a withering look. 'Oh shucks, man, don't give me that shit!'

Ronald had a bunch of lilies to give Grizelda – they looked plastic, but they weren't. But Grizelda and Portia had left a note of their own next to his: 'SO HAVE WE. BACK BY SIX.' Where had they gone?

Ronald wanted to know what the white powder was. Presumably What Every Parent Needs to Know would have told him. He went in search of Meg Shaw: Grizelda had told him she was a social worker. She ought to know.

Meg was in the middle of Chapter VIII of *Dracula*. Mina Harker was trying to work out what Lucy Westenra was doing on her night-time trips to the churchyard, with those tell-tale teeth marks on her neck. Looking up at Ronald as he loomed over her, Meg thought at first he was the insect-eating mental patient, in whose behaviour there clearly lay an important clue to everything. 'I'm sorry, you startled me.' Ronald looked at the cover of her book with some surprise. 'It's not my normal reading matter, but what are holidays for?'

'Well, actually' – he drew up a chair next to hers and sat down – 'that was what I wanted to talk to you about. What you do normally, I mean.' He looked around to make sure no one could hear them, but on one side of Meg a fat man he didn't recognize was asleep, his mouth half open and frothy bubbles waxing and waning with the rhythm of his snores. 'The manager's brother-in-law,' said Meg. On the other side, the two Joans lay equally comatose, their red toenails pointed neatly in the direction of Mecca.

'Go on,' she invited, putting her book down.

'What do you know about drugs?'

'What sort of drugs? You mean these' – she pointed at her

cigarettes – 'or that?' – Kizi passed them with a tray of drinks.

'No, I mean cannabis, and – and that sort of thing.'

She frowned at him. 'I think you'd better tell me why you want to know before I tell you what I know.'

He told her.

'Well, they grow cannabis round here. They make quite a lot of money out of it, but it's a lot cheaper than it would be in England. I don't know about the white stuff, though. Could be crack or poppers.'

'What?'

'Cocaine or amyl nitrite. You didn't see any needles, did you?'

Ronald shook his head, feeling very alarmed, and not only on Sandy's behalf either. 'I'm worried about my daughter. She's very impressionable.'

'Children are usually a good deal less impressionable than their parents think they are.' She lit a cigarette. 'I read the results of a survey done by a London University research unit the other day which showed that more parents than young people approve of drug-taking.'

Ronald's eyes widened. 'I find that hard to believe.'

'The truth often is.'

'What should we do about it, Miss Shaw?'

'It seems to me,' she said thoughtfully, 'that Joshua Holbeach is bent on self-destruction at the moment. Whatever country he's in. He's been warned – you've warned him. I'm sure his mother will as well. But we all choose our fates. To some extent,' she added, remembering Mina Harker and Dracula. 'The worst thing would be if the police got hold of Joshua.'

'Would that be the worst thing?' asked Ronald, torn between

his desire to protect Sandy Holbeach and his concern about Portia becoming a teenage junkie.

'But I doubt whether he's into hard drugs. He probably says more than he does.'

'You don't think we should contact the representative of the travel company?'

'What could she do?'

'Well, she must have come across this situation before.'

'Yes, but what could she do? I'd leave it alone myself.'

Ronald went inside to await Grizelda and Portia's return. To try to take his mind off things, he read another book he'd brought with him, on the history of the Turkish puppet theatre.

Meg tried to get back to *Dracula*, but the conversation with Ronald Dunkerley had disturbed her. Why was it that people expected her to sort out their messes even when she was on holiday? She was tired of sitting by the pool, and Aaron had gone off on his own for the day, after giving her one of his interminable lectures about smoking, the dangers of. He was threatening to give her Nicorette for Christmas. Crispin was presumably en famille, which was where he should be. She wondered idly what would happen about all of that. It was a bit like Joshua Holbeach and his mother: they'd been warned. Crispin had been warned by her. But he was an adult, which meant he was free to make his own mistakes.

Meg decided to go for a walk. But first, she'd have a shower and put some aftersun cream on those red bits. In the bathroom she fiddled with the taps for a while before realizing that no water was forthcoming. She opened her door: the Joans were passing on their way to lunch. 'Excuse me, have you had any problems with your water this morning?'

Joan number one chortled. 'Have we had any problems with our water! That's a good one, isn't it!'

Joan number two explained helpfully that the pump gave up from time to time, and this must be one of them.

Meg put the aftersun cream on anyway, and then a pale green sundress. She took her hat and purse and picked her way through Suleyman's roses to the front of the hotel. She was about to strike off in the direction of Karput when she saw the bicycles lined up outside the main entrance. It was years since she'd ridden a bike. Mehmet said she could hire one of them. She picked the nearest and set off, her green skirt flying out behind her and her sun-hat falling off her head, so she was nearly throttled by the elastic round her throat. She took the hat off and strung it over the handlebars, and gathered speed as the balancing lessons of her childhood came back to her.

Crispin Delancey thought he was seeing things when Meg and her green dress and pink cycle went past the window of the jewellery shop he was in. In front of him on the glass counter lay an array of coral, turquoise, jade, ivory and black opal necklaces. He didn't like jewellery shops, or being hassled to buy the way he was now by the young man behind the counter, who was studying part-time for an economics degree in Marmaris. Crispin was in there to buy a necklace for Dodo as a peacemaking gift, but all he could see was the slim bronzed neck of Meg Shaw. And then suddenly there was the real thing flying past the window, reflected in the counter where the stones mapped circles of precise ordered darkness. He rushed out after her: 'Meg! Stop!' The young man flew out after Crispin, afraid of losing a sale. 'Mister, you like see something cheaper? Or maybe you like some apple tea?'

She got off and came back towards him. In the midst of the

bright street, with its busy shops spilling out rugs of all kinds and colours and pottery glazed in primary reds and yellows and blues, and the clothes stalls with their silky pretend Gucci clothes, and cottons printed with flat green turtles – in the midst of all of this there was nothing brighter than Meg Shaw with her lime print dress and crinkly golden hair, like a newly fried chicken against the blue baking tray of the sky.

'Wait there!' he instructed, nipping back into the shop and, to the young man's delight, pocketing a jade necklace in return for a bagful of lire. He put it round her neck.

'I can't,' she protested, laughing.

'Why not? It's pretty, and so are you.' He grinned at her and tried to drink in the blueness of her eyes. 'Dodo's gone to call her mother from the Post Office, and then to do some shopping,' he explained. 'I'm free till supper-time. Why don't I pick up another bike and we can go for a ride?'

'I thought I'd take a look at the sulphur baths,' she said.

The road round the lake was just as spectacular as it was when Crispin and Martin Holbeach went round it the other day. In between admiring various bits of Meg's cycle-riding anatomy in front of him – the tight perimeters of her legs, the neat plum of her bottom – Crispin wondered how Martin was getting on with sorting out the politically correct position on Bosnia. Meg marvelled at the glimmery sapphire of the lake, and the pale blue of the campanula and the shocking pink of the rock-roses rising above the pale yellow stone and silver green shrubs lining the pockmarked road.

'To The Baths' said a crumbly white-fingered sign. They took a path which struck backwards and down at a forty-five degree angle to the road. Quite soon the air was heavy with sulphur. They propped up their bicycles by a military-looking hut covered in Turkish signs, and advanced round the corner. White concrete stretched to the lake, cracked and filled with flowery weeds: white camomile daisies and purple Syrian thistles, and a few islands of red-topped sage. Behind them, ranged against the rocky cliff, was a row of dingy, broken bathing huts, two-doored, with filaments of white paint still showing against the pattern of the blanched, sulphurated wood. A rectangular building on the other side carried an old metal sign which would swing in the wind if there was one: 'Home cooking. Kalte Getranke. Colddrinks. Hotel Turtle 5 minutes.' Past the bathing huts were two more buildings, each round, with a dome, and each elevated on steps above the water. Apart from the small waves lapping at the edges of the concrete, and the insects chirping in the bushes, and a few eager birds above, there was no sound at all, and there was no one here but themselves. 'How strange!' whispered Meg. 'It reminds you of one of those films about nuclear disasters, doesn't it? How long do you think it's been like this? The brochure makes it sound as though it's still a place where people come for cures. Come on, let's have a look inside.' She took his hand. Crispin would have gone anywhere attached to that hand. They climbed the steps of the first domed building. The smell of sulphur intensified. Through a corridor lined with blue-doored changing cubicles, they came to a dark round pool of hot sulphurous water with ledges for sitting on and windows without glass to let the light in. The same atmosphere lay over everything, a dense people-less odour, a stink of poison and sunlight mixed, raging weeds intermingled with sweet roses, baby terrapins outliving wild foxes, rotting material brought from the lake, and living plants rejuvenating in sunlit crevices between old Coca-Cola cans.

'I don't like this,' said Meg, pulling Crispin close to her.

'I do.' He kissed her, as though trying to obliterate the smell of sulphur by conjoining their two sun-creamed faces. He fiddled with the jade necklace with one hand and stroked her wonderful hair with the other. 'Oh Meg!' So close to him, yet so far. He kissed her neck and the reddened flesh above the top of her sundress, and then he unbuttoned it, and slid his hand inside and bent to taste her breast. It tasted of chlorine, which went with the sulphurous air. She was not trying to stop him – how could she, there was something apart from sulphur in the air here, some pulse of electricity or other energy source, something deeply biological spurring them on. She had her hands under his shirt and he had his round her waist. He felt himself urgently stick-like in front of her.

'We can't make love in a sulphur bath,' she said after a bit. She led him out, back past the white concrete ledges and into a grove of olive trees which gave some protection from the road, but let in the leaping rays of the sun. She unbuttoned her sundress and lay it down on the ground and lay him on it, and herself too.

The sun made patterns on Crispin's back as he moved in and out of Meg Shaw in tune with the perpetual dance of the waves on the land, the light on the lake, and the circles of sun, moon, earth and stars round and round in the black cavern of the universe that is all we know we have. Though they were metres away from the sulphur baths, the air around their conjugating bodies was not the normal stuff, but full of extraordinary sparkling radioactive particles. Crispin felt he could be on another planet. Meg felt the impress of the stones and earth beneath her on her sun-reddened body and the delight of the man on top as one and the same; nature and the absurdity of her creation – exactly the sort of thing one would expect to happen on a Proper Holiday.

Crispin, spent, beside her, said, 'What's that?' There was a crackling behind them in the olive grove, and a chorus of voices. Meg covered them with the skirt of her sundress, like Adam and Eve – the green of the fig leaves in the Garden of Eden, courtesy of Monsoon in Covent Garden. They lay still, hoping that whoever it was would have the vision of dinosaurs, which was activated only by movement. It was Grizelda Dunkerley and Sandy Holbeach with Portia, Primrose and Freddie. Crispin made a hurt sound like a mauled cat. Meg stuffed his t-shirt in his mouth and tried not to laugh.

'What's that?' said Sandy this time. But the olive trees screened Meg and Crispin's grotto. Portia nosed over, paralleling the edge of the white concrete and the blue lake. She stood at the edge of the spot for a moment looking silently at them, and then went away again.

'Did you see anything, darling?' asked Grizelda.

'Only a couple of goats,' said Portia. 'Chewing.'

But none of this was anything compared to the discovery Grizelda and Sandy made when they penetrated the second domed building and found in another dark circle of sulphurous water the body of one of the Welsh bird-watchers floating upside down with his binoculars dangling at the bottom of water so acrid no living weed or marine life could survive in it.

EIGHT

Master-riders in the Realm of Bliss

The Hotel Rhapsody Palas was a hive of commotion that evening, not unlike the blue bee-boxes that lined the rocky roads, wildflower pastures and boggy marshlands of the Karput coastline. As the Turkish bees hummed, making honey, so did the Turkish police, making their inquiries into the death discovered in the sulphur baths.

It was Gareth Barrett, the founder of the Cardiff section of the European Bird-watching Society. He was sixty-eight. His wife Eileen was with him. She wasn't such an ardent bird-watcher herself, and indeed on these trips spent most of her time wishing she was back in their bungalow in Lysander Road, on the outskirts of Cardiff – she'd just started an Open University arts foundation course and she was missing the television programmes. But Gareth needed his own pursuits, especially since his retirement from Messrs Bow, Latham and Barrett, Funeral Directors. He liked to come back to her with reports of triumphs spotted: 'We saw a Finsch's wheatear today, Mother,' or, 'You'll never guess, a red-fronted serin!' It was a bit like when he'd been at work and come home in the evenings with keen reports of bodies booked to be buried or cremated. People often said to Eileen, how could she bear to be married to an undertaker, a man whose hands touched the dead (by implication before they touched her, though there hadn't been much of that for a long time now). But they didn't understand it was all so clinical these days, and anyway the side of the business Gareth liked was the personal contact with the bereaved. He felt he could be helpful. At six foot three he provided a strong shoulder to cry on. Widows turned to him like trees in the wind.

Gareth had always said death was part of life, nothing to be afraid of. He was fond of quoting what the actor Sir Ralph Richardson said once: 'We don't know who we are, do we? We hardly know anyone else . . . None of us know when we are going to die . . . We're a mystery to ourselves and other people.'

Eileen said he'd gone out with the others that day in search of the gallinules – huge secretive moorhens with crimson bills that hid in reed beds. The hotel bus had taken them halfway round the lake, and they planned to walk back from there. The sulphur baths were on their route. Dai Evans reckoned they'd reached the baths at about two, but passed on quickly. 'There's no self-respecting birds'd go anywhere near that place.' According to him the radiation levels were so high, a Geiger counter would behave like a troupe of Turkish dervishes. They hadn't noticed whether Gareth was with them when they left. He often lingered, taking photographs with his new Polaroid camera.

One of the Joans, the widowed one, gave Eileen some tranquillizers. 'I know what it's like,' she sympathized, 'though mine died in hospital of cancer of the leg. It hasn't really hit you yet, but it will do.'

Eileen sobbed and shrieked, 'If it hasn't hit me yet, what will I feel like when it does?' All the bird-watchers and their partners gathered round her protectively like a flock of birds round one that's injured. She sobbed until the tranquillizers sent her to sleep on Joan's bed. Before that, she wasn't much good as a source of information to the police, except about her own guilt in not being as nice to Gareth over the years as she should have been. Through the veil of her distress, episodes of putative unkindness peeked like ferns through a waterfall: the time she'd roared at him, shortly after his retirement, for saying for the nth time, what are we going to do today, Mother?; the way she'd made him keep all his bird-watching equipment in a special cupboard instead of out at the ready as he would have liked; the times she'd viciously made haddock for supper when she was cross with him, knowing full well he'd fancy a steak and kidney pie or lamb chops with fat browned like the feathers of a baby sparrow. But on the other hand, these reactions of hers were not because of nothing. In some ways, Gareth hadn't been a perfect husband. He had this habit of going out for a few hours and not saying where he went. She put it down to his hormones – she preferred that as an explanation to thinking he had a secret life. Oh Gareth Barrett, what sins of miscommunication may never be discovered now you're dead!

A post-mortem would be done. They had one son, a songwriter who lived in California. Gareth had wanted Lloyd to go into the family business, but there was no way he was going to do that – he went off and wrote songs about death instead. Dai telephoned Lloyd and told him what had happened. He hadn't seen either of his parents for five years. He'd definitely come back to Cardiff for the funeral, and would probably write a few songs about it.

The police interviewed everyone in the hotel, beginning with Mehmet and the rest of the staff and then working systematically through the guests. The maids were cross to be kept behind, as they were already late because of having to bail out Miss Shaw's room. It had flooded when the water came back on because she'd left the taps open; her red shoes and *Dracula* had floated on a tide right over the balcony.

People sat around in groups talking in deadened voices. Every little patio held a huddle of them nursing glasses of brandy or cups of tea or coffee. There was a run on the Earl Grey teabags and Kizi had to ask Bilge to go into Karput and get some more. In the middle of all this, Martin Holbeach arrived back, claiming to have solved the problem of *Socialism Now*'s editorial line on Bosnia. Star Delancey and Wilma Blake looked meaningfully at one another. 'What was the weather like in England, Mr Holbeach?' inquired Star. Dodo and Crispin couldn't understand why she was suddenly interested in the weather.

So who would be suspected of causing Gareth Barrett's death? Three theories received some support: one, some manic local Turkish predator, either randomly murderous or bent on killing off tourists; two, someone military, who considered Gareth with all his watching equipment a spy of some kind; and, three, one of the bird-watchers themselves.

Carly Atkins, she of Proper Holidays who was supposed to be looking after this crowd, arrived in the hotel about the same time as Martin Holbeach; in fact it was she who explained to him why the forecourt was littered with police cars. Carly was cross at having to give up her evening, as she'd been planning to spend it with a strapping blond Dutchman from a travel company in The Hague. It was his first summer here and she wanted to show him the ropes. He'd got a Vauxhall Senator company car and they'd been thinking of going into Ocakkoy to the new Turkish baths there, which did mixed sex massages, and then to the new fish restaurant in the hills, and then after that if they still had any wind in their sails, Carly had intended to take him to a disco. She'd planned the evening down to the last detail. Even what she was going to wear – her blue silk dress, which was tight in all the important places, and a brass choker and shoes as high and white as the cliffs of Dover. So it was all the more frustrating in view of the fact that Matt was in immense demand. Carly's throat constricted and threatened another infection at the thought of Hilda, the German rep at Matt's hotel, using this evening as an opportunity to get her own claws into him.

Gareth Barrett, along with the rest of the bird-watchers, had been a Proper Holidays client. But Carly couldn't even remember what he looked like – they'd arrived en masse at Karaman two weeks ago, a crowd of oldish chaps and their wives and other hangers-on with a lot of green anoraks and binocular cases. She'd ticked their names off on a list, but that was different from matching faces to them. She hadn't had a death before. Most experienced reps would have had at least one, along with the normal miscarriages, appendicitises, mental breakdowns, chickenpoxes, fractured limbs, marital disputes, and the heartless heart attacks of relatives left behind.

'What am I supposed to do, Kizi?'

'Talk to Mrs Barrett first, and the police. Then there will be the question of how to get the body home. After that it might be a good idea if you spoke to everyone. There's been quite a lot going on around here.'

The police weren't very interested in Carly, and nor was Mrs Barrett. 'What would you know about death?' she asked accusingly, and rightly. 'You're not even married, are you?' Dai Evans seemed to have taken charge. There'd be no body to be flown anywhere anyway until the post-mortem had been done.

Carly chalked a notice on the blackboard in reception: 'Special meeting of Proper Holiday clients. By the bar at 6.30 tonight.'

'What do you mean, "quite a lot's been going on around here", Kizi?'

'This year the enjoyment has got out of hand. The young people, they stay out late, they take boats where they shouldn't, they buy liquor when they shouldn't. They make a mess in their rooms. They smoke hash-hash.'

'But they're just a bunch of kids,' Carly said, referring to the young people. 'Wild about nothing. Like we were at their age.'

'I wasn't,' he observed gravely. 'But I think this is a cultural difference, perhaps.' Kizi remembered when he was young: the simple mud-brick village houses on the flat Anatolian plain: hot in summer, with a winter landscape dominated by the white caps of mountains. When he was a boy, the women still wore the traditional Anatolian dress – bright billowy panta-loons, blouses and sleeveless vests with a *çarşat* over their hair. Since Atatürk, the young women had left their faces uncovered, but his grandmother had stuck to the old custom. Then the reaping had been done by women using traditional sickles; scythes, used by men, came in later. European ploughs began to replace the old ox-ploughs about the same time. Even now his parents continued to regard the new ways with some sus-picion. After all, didn't they have a habit of disturbing the old values, such as the division of tasks between men and women ordained by Allah? In Kizi's parents' house there was a men's room still – a place at the back with some worn-out couches and bright rugs where the men of the village gathered, and the women were not allowed. If the men wanted anything when they were there, they sent one of the boys out for it. There had been seven of them in a three-room house: him, his parents, three brothers and a sister. One of his brothers lived there still, with his wife and son; the others lived near. Only Kizi had left to earn his living elsewhere. But this didn't mean he was rejecting his roots. He couldn't understand why anyone would want to do this. Of course, not every old tradition was good – his father was fond of telling him about the ceremony of circumcision when the Sünnetei came and talked to you teasingly and then with a flick of his knife before you knew what was happening whipped off your foreskin. So not everything was good, but there was always a point to it, and everyone was part of it, you knew where you belonged.

'It'd be a dull world if we were all the same, wouldn't it?' observed Carly. 'These young people aren't doing any harm, are they? I mean apart from the hash-hash, and a few hangovers and rows with their parents, and so forth.'

Kizi was not to be deterred by Carly's downgrading of all this to teenage antics. 'There is something bad going on here,' he continued. 'There is some bad influence at work. I am not surprised we have had a death.'

'Well, I am. Don't be so melodramatic.'

'Melodramatic?'

'You're making too much of a fuss about it.' Carly thought Kizi a bit of an oddball. At first she'd suspected him of being queer, but then Mehmet had told her about Zephra. Kizi did his job well, but he thought about things too much. Her own philosophy was not to think overmuch. There was no point in trying to understand the meaning of things.

147

'It's not just the young people. It's their parents, too.'

Carly sighed. She'd had enough of this.

'One of the men said he had to go home on business, but he didn't. His wife is having an affair with the husband of another one. The husband of another one is having an affair with another woman, who doesn't have a husband.'

'Well, that's crystal clear, I'm sure.'

'One of the ladies buries her food by the roses, and two of the other ladies got food poisoning.'

'Where did they get it from? Not here, I hope?'

'No, from Kovzli's carpet shop.'

'Well, what can you expect?' She swung round on her bar stool a couple of times. 'It all sounds quite normal to me. This is a business, Kizi, you have to take what you get.' She remembered this being said to all of them in head office, on their four-day induction course. 'Though I'm not sure about the buried food. Maybe you imagined that? And romances are one of the things people come on holiday for.'

Kizi looked puzzled. 'Why do they come with their families, then?'

'I suppose they can hardly leave them behind.'

Nearly everyone turns up at six thirty for Carly's talk. Sandy Holbeach is plastered again (or still) and confused as to whether she's glad Martin is back or not. Ronald Dunkerley is worrying about Portia and the white powder. Derrick and Lisa Upton are crisply dressed for dinner, and Wilma Blake has her newspaper under her arm just in case. Crispin Delancey is pink and damp from the shower, and Dodo wears a look more worried than usual, and a gaudy new skirt bought in Karput that afternoon while her husband and Meg, whose current demeanour gives nothing away, were screwing in the olive grove. The honeymooners come flushed with post-coital hormones, and a clever plan for the bar area in their starter's sitting room. The two Joans sit either side of Dai with the other bird-watchers behind like crows on a field waiting for the picking. Of the young people, Jade and Star, Portia and Aaron are there, the former under instruction from their parents, Portia because she thinks it's all like some exciting detective story, or an episode out of one of the paperbacks she's discovered in the hotel reception, and Aaron because it's in his nature. Kelly and Simon have been told to stay with Stevie and Primrose and Freddie (Sandy would have told Josh to stay with his siblings himself had he been around to tell). They're all in one of the Uptons' rooms with colouring books and Stevie's Nintendo games. Kelly's on the balcony reading a Mills & Boon.

Only Grizelda Dunkerley is unaccounted for. She's lying in her room with the curtains drawn. It's partly the shock of seeing the back of a dead man in a sulphur pool, and partly that she's overdosed on kaolin and is now suffering from the opposite complaint of totally bunged-up bowels.

'Well, now,' says Carly trying to be cheerful, 'can I offer anyone a drink?'

'What we want to know,' says Derrick Upton, proprietorially, and ignoring Carly's mollifying offer, 'is what's going on here?'

'The police are investigating Mr Barrett's death,' says Carly primly.

'I know, I know, but don't you think it's a bit funny, this chap keeling over in the sulphur baths when certain other people' – he casts an unfairly meaningful glance at Sandy Holbeach – 'have been, well, mixing with a criminal element? I don't know whether anybody else has noticed,' he went on, 'that gang of youths who've been hanging around the front of the hotel in the last few days. One of them was a soldier. He had a gun.' Derrick stops for effect.

'Oh, Mr Upton, don't let's get things out of proportion!'

'It's like a news story in the *Daily Mail*, isn't it?' observes Wilma Blake helpfully.

'No, it isn't,' objects Martin Holbeach. 'You don't want to believe anything you read in that rag.'

'Aren't we getting rather off the point here?' suggests Ronald Dunkerley.

'It *is* the point, Mr – Professor, whoever you are. Didn't they want skills in logical deduction when they made you a professor? Someone round here needs to put two and two together.'

'And make five,' finishes Meg Shaw. 'I agree with Professor Dunkerley. We should all calm down and just let the police get on with their job.'

One of the Joans opens her mouth to say something, but the other one speaks instead. 'It's your young people,' she says. 'They are quite a bother, aren't they?'

'Yes they are,' says the first one quietly. 'Exactly what I was going to say.'

'What do you mean, "quite a bother"?' asks Jade from the back row. No one thought she'd even been listening; she's been fiddling with her extensions like a cat with its tail. 'Has it ever occurred to you, Mrs or Miss or *Miz*' – she pauses threateningly on this last suggestion – 'that we young people find you old ones quite a bother too, with all your complaints and narrow-mindedness and not wanting anyone to enjoy themselves and going to sleep at ten o'clock and expecting everyone else to do the same and hanging your nasty white cotton knickers all over your balconies and wanting to listen to classical music all the time?'

'Shush,' says Dodo anxiously. 'Please, Jade, not now!'

'I don't even like classical music!' complains Joan. 'Well, we didn't mind the show of Pavarotti singing in Central Park, did we, Joan? But on the whole we prefer musicals, you know, *Cats* and *Joseph and his Multi-coloured Dreamcoat* and so forth, and Barry Manilow.'

'Off the point again!' shouts Ronald like a cricket umpire.

'I've got to go in a minute,' says Carly dishonestly. 'I'm afraid,' she adds quickly, 'I promised I'd call in at the Ocakkoy villas before dinner.' That should give her time to intercept Hilda. They none of them knew what they were talking about. They shouldn't be talking about anything anyway, they should all be lying back layered in aftersun cream beside the pool with their G-and-Ts while Kizi lit the pool lights and the mosquitoes came out for their night-time feed and the waiters went round with cans of chemical spray. Whatever way you looked at it, it was all death and destruction anyway – either of mosquitoes or of men or of dreams.

She gets up to go. They look at her as if she's a mother abandoning them, far from home in a nasty foreign place neither she nor they understand. 'I'm sorry,' she says inanely, though she isn't, at all. 'I'm sure things'll settle down. You don't any of you look like murderers to me.'

After Carly had gone, Wilma Blake passes round the pictures of Fergie and her financial adviser to lighten the mood. 'I feel sorry for her, I really do. She's entitled to a bit of happiness. Though what she sees in that one' – she points a stumpy finger at a picture of John Bryan with his mouth open on page three – 'is beyond me. He's got even less hair than the Prince! I expect he makes up for it in other departments,' she adds darkly.

The two Joans giggle and pore over Mrs Blake's shoulder at the hazy coloured pictures. 'The one of the detective is particularly incriminating,' Wilma adds helpfully. 'I hope the Turkish police are more on their mettle than that, or they'll never solve the riddle of poor Mr Barrett's death. D'you think I could have a gin and lime, Derrick?'

She seems unusually gay.

'Of course, Mother.'

'Talking of mothers,' goes on Wilma, even more gaily, 'there's a piccy of the Queen in there, you'll find it towards the end. She's looking quite sour on a horse. I don't expect she understands that what her daughter-in-law is doing is done by lots of other people in that country of hers, it's just that most of them don't have long range cameras trained on them while they're doing it.' She dips into her gin and lime with every appearance of innocence.

'There's free wine tonight for all of you,' announces Kizi. 'We have laid the tables together on the terrace by the river.' Mehmet had decided they needed to take steps to remedy the reputation of his hotel. Kizi didn't approve of the free alcohol, but he did think it a good idea that the Uptons and Delanceys and Dunkerleys and Holbeaches and the Joans and the remaining bird-watchers be encouraged to find in one another that basic human camaraderie most of them seemed to have forgotten.

'Derrick'll bring his video, won't you, Derrick,' promises Lisa, trying to enter into the spirit of things. It isn't dark yet, but the sun has dropped behind the rock tombs, and the river is hung with pinkish light. The tourist boats cut measured patterns across its hard clear surface, like crystal glasses full of rosé wine. The boats come back from the salty stretches of Turtle Beach, and from the stinking bogs of the mud baths, and from the effervescent air of Lake Dinya, where Martin Holbeach had urinated on the back of a swimming turtle and, had he lived, Gareth Barrett of Lysander Road, Cardiff, would have gone next week in search of rare and pleasing birds. In the town of Karput, tourists in the cheap Pansiyons take their places in the harbourside cafés for their plates of *spagety bolonez* and *lamp spit*. In the police station Denzli Jarmu of the Karaman district police has a glass of beer and studies his list of suspects, for all the world unlike Hercule Poirot. In the back room of a bar by the campsite on the coast road out of Karput sits Joshua Holbeach with Yusuf and Celik and Celik's girlfriend Tansil. An old Cliff Richard is playing in the background. Joshua is drinking vodka, the others Coke. He's feeling hungry and also, though he wouldn't want to admit it, in need of a shower. They slept last night on the beach. He did go back to the hotel once to look for Jade, but he gave up at the thought of having to prise her away from her goody-goody sister. Joshua drums the rhythm of the song on the table. He's bored. But that's not unusual.

In the Hotel Rhapsody Palas now the air is still; no breeze from the sea moves the singing grasses by the river, or the clumps of red hibiscus, and all the yellow and orange and red and white roses stare with their open honest faces out into the close night air like an audience waiting for the evening performance to start.

Eileen Barrett will eat, or rather not eat, in her room, and so will the bird-watchers who knew Gareth well. Everyone else arranges themselves at the tables by the river. 'We're not sitting with the rest of them, are we?' asks Kelly anxiously. She and Jade and Star and Aaron and Simon take over one of the smaller tables. Portia sits down with them. 'All right,' says Kelly, 'but we're not having the *real* babies.'

To make the proceedings simple, Mehmet has decreed a limited choice menu – in fact two per course. Star doesn't want any of them, as they all include animal protein or green cooked things, and Grizelda Dunkerley, who has slunk out from her room clutching her stomach on husband Ronald's insistence, wants something that is truly lubricating, such as two litres of olive oil.

'Don't worry, dear,' says Wilma Blake comfortingly, 'you can have some of my Senokot. It goes from one extreme to the other, doesn't it?'

'Where is Joshua?' asks Martin threateningly, as he was bound to sooner or later. Sandy, who is sitting opposite him, occupies herself tying a napkin round young Freddie's neck. She sips her cool bean soup and feels the next hot flush about to start. 'You heard me, Sandy, where is he?'

'I've no idea,' she says. 'None at all.' It's going to be a bad one. Her ears seem to be ringing with something, and droplets of sweat are altering the temperature of her soup.

'When did you last see him?'

'Yesterday morning.'

'So where was he last night?'

'I told you, I haven't got a clue.'

'Jesus Christ! I go away for a couple of days, and I come back to find a murder, and my son's missing and nobody seems the least bit concerned, especially not his own mother!'

'Well, perhaps you shouldn't have gone away, then,' suggests Dodo gently. Crispin looks at her in surprise.

'What?'

'I only meant that when you come away on a family holiday it's up to everyone to make sure it's a success, isn't it?'

'You think it's *my* fault I had to go back to bloody London, do you?'

'Please, Martin!' Sandy's hot flush has gone, and now she's started to shiver.

'Please Martin what?'

'I'm going to say something I'll regret soon,' whispers Meg Shaw to Crispin.

Ronald Dunkerley looks at them suspiciously, and then guiltily at his own wife, who is tinkering with the frills of some octopus. 'You all right, dear?'

'Oh yes, Ronald.'

'Do you think you ought to check on Portia? It looks to me as though they've got some wine on their table.'

'Does it really matter, Ronald?' Grizelda looks abnormally pale, and so does Sandy, now her hot flush is over. Ronald looks round the table at all these pale women.

'Family, shamily,' says Martin Holbeach, refilling his wine glass. 'You women have no idea what it's like for us men these days. You're so full of your own emancipation you've totally failed to notice that it's men who are enslaved. We're the ones who've got to keep the whole bloody caboodle going. Go to work, to jobs we hate, for fifty years just in order to pay the bills – the school bills, the doctor's bills, the dentist's bills, the garage bills, the grocery bills, the hairdresser's bills, the new sofas and the carports and the microwaves and the burglar alarms and the double-action cat doors – we pick up the tab for everything so you women don't have to work. Oh, I know you've all got part-time jobs – but those are hobbies, really. The world wouldn't come to an end if you gave them up. As a matter of fact, it'd help, then there'd be more jobs for us men. And don't tell me that looking after kids is work. You can lie around all day with your feet up watching TV while the little darlings run amok and bring themselves up to be people like Josh.' He empties his glass with a flourish, and looks around for another bottle.

Sandy closes her eyes and leans back in her chair. Down the table Beverley and her young man hold on to one another under the tablecloth vowing that they will never be like Sandy and Martin Holbeach. Lisa Upton fingers the silver cross round her neck urgently, and would have a hot flush in sympathy with Sandy Holbeach if her body allowed her to.

But it's Derrick Upton who takes up Martin Holbeach's challenge. 'I think you should watch your words, Holbeach. There are ladies present. Opinions such as those you've just voiced went out with the ark. Women have as much right to jobs as men. And if you think looking after kids isn't work, that can only be because you've never tried it. Perhaps if you'd done more in that department your son would be here now sitting decently with the others.' He throws a glance towards the table at the end where his daughter Kelly is currently engaged in killing a tree frog with a jar of toothpicks. 'As for that stuff about all the bills you have to pay, if you were a decent Labour voter instead of a half-baked leftie you'd be supporting the state educational system and the National Health Service which would cut your expenditure in half!'

Mehmet, who has come out to check on the proceedings, sees that his plan has misfired. He stands behind one of Suleyman's roses in the darkness watching. Round the scent of the rose a clan of hawk moths fly, the purple of their wings flashing like the jewels in the shops of Karput. In the bushes round the low wall male fireflies light their tips and SOS for females, whose weaker illumination may signal either biological accident or a disinclination to mate. Mehmet enjoys showing the fireflies to the clients of his hotel, but he's not brave enough to interrupt the flow of talk round the tables at the moment.

'You're right, of course,' says Martin Holbeach unexpectedly after Derrick's speech. 'Well, not about the education and health services, but we can talk about those later. I'm overwrought. I'm probably worried about Josh, sod the little bugger, and about the fate of Bosnia-Herzegovina.'

'It isn't easy living in families.' Meg Shaw lights a cigarette, but will not be mistaken for a willing female by any firefly.

'Do you know anything better?' Lisa Upton thinks of the little children in her primary school reception class, all calling her 'Mum', all needy and innocent and trusting.

'In traditional Turkish culture,' supplies Ronald Dunkerley, uninvited, 'there's no recognition of the nuclear family as the primary building unit of society. Historically speaking, the main social group has always been the wider family, the three-generation family, with sons never leaving their fathers in their fathers' lifetimes, and taking their wives and children to live with them.'

'God forbid!' says Martin Holbeach weakly, thinking of Josh never leaving his side, though there must be a happy medium between being there all the time and never being there at all.

'As a matter of fact, there's not even a word for "family" in the language,' adds Ronald as an afterthought. It had struck him as a contrast: the importance of kinship and locality in traditional Turkish culture, and the mess the visitors were all making of trying to be happy nuclear families. He includes himself in this. He hopes Sandy has forgotten his pale body and drooping genitalia skinny-dipping the other night. He hopes Portia hasn't said anything to her mother. He hopes she isn't being corrupted, as he has been, by the company they're keeping.

'Look at us,' Martin says expansively, himself looking around at this company assembled round the table by the river Dinacek in southern Turkey through the accident of having got hold of the Proper Holidays summer 1992 brochure. 'Look at us: we're all professional people, well, in one way or another,' he adds, noticing Derrick Upton at the edge of his vision. 'Think of all the professional training and experience we've got between us, and look at what good it does us when it comes to sorting these young people out!'

No one says they agree with him, which doesn't mean they don't.

'What about you, Miss Shaw, you're a social worker, I understand. What makes good parents, do you think? And do you think good parents make good children, or doesn't it work like that?'

'Being a social worker doesn't give me the answers to every-thing, Mr Holbeach.'

'Doesn't it? I thought that was exactly what it gave you.'

'The fact that some people,' Sandy Holbeach says defensively at this point, and throwing a studied look in Meg's direction, 'have kids who don't give them problems doesn't mean a thing. It's got nothing to do with how good a parent you are.'

'Social workers make me sick!' Martin Holbeach is getting truly stuck into his theme now. 'Behind all your modern talk, you're all Victorian charity workers with holier-than-thou atti-tudes. I've got news for you, Miss Shaw. You're not. Holier than me. Or any of us. What do you think, Delancey?'

Crispin has been trying to occupy himself with fishing a fly out of his wine, but all he's succeeded in doing is squashing it up against the side of the glass and removing its wings. He hadn't wanted to say anything because it'd look as though he were defending Meg, which he would be, and that could upset Dodo, and then things might really get out of hand. 'I think we all do our best,' he said eventually and inanely.

One of the Joans speaks up suddenly. 'My aunt – whom I'm named after – she had six children, and I remember her saying to my mother, who only had me, that the best way to bring up children was to lay off.'

'I don't agree!' Meg bristles at this. 'Children deserve and need all the attention they can get. Indeed, from that point of view the main problem is that in most families they have to compete for attention. They've got the marital relationship to contend with, for starters.'

Unsurprisingly, Sandy Holbeach disagrees. 'But coming to terms with the Oedipal relationship's a necessary condition for mental health!'

'Is it? I think you'll find most people don't believe in Oedipus any more.'

'That's neither here nor there.'

'As a matter of fact it is. It's one of the reasons why the children of single mothers often do better psychologically than those in two-parent families.'

'That's a load of crap! Everyone knows that children need two parents!' Derrick Upton leaps into the fray.

'Well, in one way yes, they need as many parents as they can get. But who needs a father who abuses his children or beats his partner, and who needs men who are so busy thinking about their own egos they don't even notice other people's needs?' There was a stunned silence. 'All right, all right, I knew I shouldn't have said that. I take it all back. I'm only a social worker on holiday. Pass me a cigarette, someone!'

Everyone in the Hotel Rhapsody Palas has their own theories, hopes, fears and dreams, but only a few dare admit even the barest outlines of these. On their table under the Mediterranean night sky, drowning their tastebuds in chocolate mousse, Star and Aaron Shaw talk about the way her dad and his mum are getting off with each other. 'It's not so bad for you,' observes Star. 'Your mother isn't married.'

'But do I want you for a sister?' asks Aaron rhetorically. There are tears in Star's eyes. 'By the way, why are you called Star?'

'My father said there was a star over the Royal Free Hospital the night I was born.'

'Like Jesus.' Star laughs through her tears. 'Don't cry. I'm out of the Bible, too. Strange, isn't it, the way they turn to religion to name us, when they turn away from it the rest of the time? Don't worry, we'll find a way to defeat them.'

Further up the big table Dodo tries to see past her neighbours to check out what her daughter Star is, or is not, eating. Lisa tells Dodo of her search through the pharmacies of Karput for something effective with which to dissipate Kelly's prickly heat rash, and in the process is seen by mother-in-law Wilma Blake, who is sitting opposite, to shift half the food on her plate into a six-by-four freezer bag secreted in her white linen handbag. Wilma recommends the leaves of a local plant for Kelly's rash. 'Old wives' tales, Mum,' says Lisa curtly.

'Old wives' tales'll do you far better than young husbands' ones!'

'I think that woman knows things we don't,' observes Meg Shaw to Crispin.

He reaches out a hand for a bare, delicious knee under the table: 'You will come with me to an olive grove again one day, won't you?'

Behind the yellow rose, Mehmet thinks of the truth of the saying that fortunate people are not the ones who have everything, but those who know the value of what they've got. At the head of the table, Professor Ronald Dunkerley leans back and looks beyond the lights of Karput out into the blackness of the open sea. It all seems very far away from the world of the university and final degrees and appraisal schemes and research selectivity exercises, and the outrageous but ultimately trivial vagaries of the Higher Education Funding Council. And although it isn't quite the holiday they thought they were getting, he must admit it's a change. Suddenly a phrase from a Turkish poem by Baki (1527–1600) comes into his head. Baki is describing the death of Sultan Suleyman the Magnificent in 1566, which had been a great personal blow. Baki calls Suleyman a 'master-rider in the realm of bliss'. Ronald supposes that's what they are all trying to be, though variously failing, as few human beings can achieve Suleyman's magnificence. 'Think of that day when, at the end of the spring of life,' murmurs Ronald to the blackness, himself thinking of the seductions of the realms of earthly bliss and the suddenness of death sprung in sulphur pools on the likes of Eileen Barrett: 'The tulip-coloured face will turn into an autumn leaf. / For you, as for the dregs in the cup, earth must be the last dwelling; / The stone from the hand of time must strike the cup of life.'

NINE

The Rubbish Heap of Knowledge

Ronald Dunkerley mused about the differences between similar experiences. A holiday wasn't just a holiday. Indeed, it very often wasn't at all. He wondered about the meaning of the word. If he'd been at home, he would have looked it up in the 26-volume *OED* they kept in what he called the library and Grizelda called the front room. It was a front room, but it did have a lot of books in it, including his own three and Grizelda's six, of which her *The Sacred and the Vernacular in Early English Writing* was the best known, having quite unintentionally (on her part) been published at a time – 1979 – when the media were still eager to refute or confirm the idea that women could be just like men (one of its themes was the general invisibility of women writers). Grizelda was a dreadful teacher – her students all said so, and most of them got third-class degrees. She had a habit of mumbling, so you only picked up the odd word here and there, and of forgetting large parts of the syllabus, especially the American novel and most of the twentieth century. On the other hand, she was very good on her specialist area, and there had been a few students who'd dragged themselves up to 2:1s on this basis, and even gone on to do Ph.D.s, though this hadn't done them an awful lot of good, as there wasn't much call for people who specialized in early English writing.

'Holiday': originally 'holy day'. A day of festivity or rec-
reation when no work is done. Holidays, once defined by
religion, had become secular events principally distinguished
from others by the obligation *not to work*. This implied that
work itself was a distasteful, tiring activity. Work was what you
had to do to earn money so you could pay the bills. And afford
holidays. The whole thing then became circular: you needed
a holiday from work, but you had to work to have a holiday.
As with everything, an historical perspective could be useful
here: what history taught was that the underlying issue was
men's relationship to labour.

It also mattered who you worked *for*. Ronald counted himself
lucky that he worked for a university, as until recently this had
enabled him to believe he worked for himself. In other words,
although there were the students, the departmental meetings,
and other administrative matters to attend to, his chief duty
was to bring his mental capacities to bear on and advance the
understanding of history. It was his responsibility to ensure
that the investment his parents and country had made in his
education was not wasted, and that by thought and diligent
reading and pursuit of specific historical questions over time
he would bring into the world a little more knowledge than
had been there when he joined it.

Ronald thought of knowledge as a finite thing: in his mind
it was a heap, rather like the household refuse tip near where
they lived, and on to which people put things they had once
owned, so that the mound grew and parts of it flaked off and
were carried through the air to reach other parts which had
previously lain bare. The heap of knowledge in Ronald's head
was a dark orange, unlike the rubbish dump which was multi-
coloured, though on this it was the white elements that attracted

one's attention as one drove past and which the local residents tended most to complain about, since they had the habit of fluttering unlike doves into their front and back gardens. Mental images, reflected Ronald, are often coloured; words, flat and ordinary in themselves, give rise to multi-dimensional and multi-tinctured visions. 'Holiday' – now 'holiday' is green; green and rather undistinguished in shape, like the fluorescent protoplasm in ghost stories, forming and re-forming its globules under the influence of different characters in the afterlife. Do they have holidays in heaven or is heaven a holiday? In which case, what happens in hell? Ronald made a mental note to pursue this theme when he got home.

Ronald would have liked to discuss some of this with Sandy Holbeach, as he thought her professional expertise as a therapist might help him to understand it. He did feel an increasing need to understand things these days. As you got older, you thought about the past more, and became more and more aware of the ways in which it influenced you. That was one of the reasons he'd been keen to take up Perkins' suggestion and bring his daughter to a more historic part of the world for her holidays than Cornwall. He wanted Portia to understand how we are all mere atoms in the great relentless march of civilization, which rises and falls and heaves and changes rather like the green protoplasm of ghost stories, or the word 'holiday' itself, and irrespective of what individual human beings themselves think might be going on, or ought to be. He himself had gained a real sense of that the other day when they'd gone to Punka, the site Perkins had recommended for its necropolis and unfluted columns. The city had been laid out on the Hippodamic system. A strict geometric design meant that streets intersected at right angles. However, because it was built on a hill, they also had to be stepped, sometimes by as much as thirty-three degrees. You could see the remains of an extensive underground system of clay pipes providing water and carrying away waste. The Cnidians had been very civilized. Not only had they had a sewage system, but a medical school and several theatres, and then Eudoxus (400–347 BC) had built himself an observatory so he could observe the star Canopus properly night after night, and Praxiteles had sculpted Aphrodite, which Pliny thought was one of the Wonders of the World, and which people everywhere had copied ever since – Ronald remembered his own mother using the emblem of the armless woman in some of her paintings. It must have been a wonderful place, Cnidus, in Roman times. But then in the Byzantine period it had declined, and by the Middle Ages it had been abandoned altogether. Ronald didn't believe in the thesis of dialectical materialism, which seemed to him to have elements in common with simple Darwinian evolutionism. Nothing got better and better all the time. Much of history was, in any case, sheer accident. For example, had the Captain of HMS *Beagle* not decided to take a naturalist on board for a change, Charles Darwin himself might never have had the opportunity to notice the way that things tended to evolve. The point was that all these great sweeps of history both contained and added up to more than the sums of the individuals who composed them. Take Praxiteles now: he could not have been aware that the sophisticated culture of which he was a part would be overthrown by relative barbarism, nor could he possibly have predicted the role of his Aphrodite as a cultural artefact and metaphor in subsequent quite different civilizations. But, as well as history sweeping individuals along in its overwhelming tides, there is a sense in which everything can also ultimately be reduced to individual experience. Praxiteles made the statue of Aphrodite because he was in love with a woman. He wanted to make her and their love transcendent by putting it into stone.

When he'd explained all this to Portia, who took some of it in and at least understood why numbers went backwards Before Christ, unlike some of her peers in state schools, he'd seen her looking at him oddly. Was it because she thought he was only going on about Aphrodite as a result of his encounters with Sandy Holbeach? Sandy was no Aphrodite. Aphrodite had clearly been a large lady, and Sandy was a small one. Sandy seemed to be rather frightened by experience, whereas all the signs were that Aphrodite had embraced it, much as the vast theatre of Cnidus had seemed to hold the blue half moon of the Aegean Sea in its generous sculpted curve.

It would have been nice to have had a great love. A love of the kind that Praxiteles had enjoyed with his Aphrodite, and Ronald Dunkerley might have found with Sandy Holbeach. A love that consumed you, and carried you along with it, like the oceanic tides of history.

Ronald was sitting on the patio of their room with Grizelda. 'This is the worst holiday I've ever had,' said Grizelda. 'I've been ill and you've been – well, odd. And then Portia lost her glasses and that Welshman died. I'm not convinced they know how to make glasses in Turkey. We should have gone to Cornwall, like we always do.'

'Yes, dear.'

'I blame Perkins. It was all his idea, wasn't it?'

'Yes. But if you remember, we did feel it was a bit dull always going to Cornwall. There were mice the last time.'

'I'd rather have mice than all this. I don't know what effect it's all going to have on Portia. Just think what might have happened if she hadn't been younger than them!' she invited. Grizelda's main feature as a mother was her concern about contamination. When Portia was younger Grizelda's fear of contamination had focused on Portia's bodily system, and had expressed itself principally as a worry about viruses, headlice, diseases of the skin and anal worms. Now it was her behaviour. Would association with the likes of Joshua Holbeach, Jade and Star Delancey, Kelly and Simon Upton, and the other comrades they'd found among the native Karput youth, induce in Portia unpleasant, antisocial behaviour of new kinds, whose form and consequences lay beyond the limits of Grizelda's precisely focused literary imagination? What if Portia had teenage sex (it would be difficult for her to have any other sort), or took up cannabis-smoking, or did any of those things that Grizelda, like Ronald, hadn't read about in What Every Parent Needs to Know? What if she stopped eating or started being very rude to her parents like Jade Delancey, or, even worse, like Joshua Holbeach? What if she stopped being ready to wear the plain untasteful clothes selected for her by Grizelda, and went in for horrible unpolished boots and body-revealing grey-edged broderie anglaise instead? What if holes appeared in her ears, or, worse still, in other places? What if she demanded one of those personal music machines, or contact lenses, or, later on, when her periods started, which Grizelda vainly hoped they never would, vaginal tampons and the pill?

'I don't think I can cope with it all,' said Grizelda weakly. Ronald had heard that before, and she was usually right.

Like the Delanceys' patio further along, the Dunkerleys' looked out on the tall river grasses and the Angela Rippon roses which hid the ploughing of the boats back and forth to Turtle

Beach. What was the point of knowledge, after all? What if the orange heap got bigger and bigger without anything else happening, without any bits of it flaking off and flying through the air to arrive as unsolicited gifts on people's front lawns – or, if they didn't have these, as Ronald imagined some people almost certainly didn't, living as they almost certainly must in mean little council houses – in their front rooms, which really were front rooms, and not, as in the Dunkerleys' case, really libraries?

'Where is Portia, anyway?' asked Grizelda, from behind the restricted view on their patio. 'I hope she's not off doing anything she shouldn't.'

'She said she was going to see if there were any interesting books in reception.'

Portia had discovered Mills & Boon, courtesy of Kelly Upton, thus confirming all her father's worst class hatred, and was at that very moment holding in her hand one called *Steps to Heaven*, which featured on its front cover a terribly thin young woman in a strapless silver dress with her arms round a tall dark handsome Cary Grant look-alike. She'd already read *A Question of Pride*, *Prisoner*, *Flight of Discovery* and *Unfriendly Alliance*, although all of these had been inserted between the covers of her history book, so her parents wouldn't notice.

Jade and Star were having an argument just outside the main door of the hotel. 'Well, I don't think we should,' said Star. 'It's not fair. They'll worry.'

'You nerd, that's just the point! It's time they did worry about something that's worth worrying about! It's only for a day or two. Just to frighten them. We'll have some fun, too. I'm fed up with this dump, aren't you? Nothing ever happens here.'

The child Portia looked up from *Steps to Heaven*. That didn't seem quite right, as someone had just died here. She got up and went outside. 'Can I come with you? Please! I'm bored too.'

They looked her up and down scathingly. 'Come where? We're not going anywhere!'

Portia retreated. Wilma Blake came in and sat down. Portia studied the book in her lap, but her eyes were misted with tears.

'They won't let me go with them,' she mumbled.

'Who won't?'

'Jade and Star.'

'Well, don't take it to heart, dearie, they're older than you. I expect they've got things to do in town. Where are your parents?'

'In our room arguing. They're not very interested in me really. My dad says my mum's neurotic. What does "neurotic" mean? My mum doesn't really like anything except her work. She's a professor, you know. She writes books about books. You'd think there were enough books in the world already, wouldn't you, Mrs Blake?'

'You would, you would.' Wilma laughed. If only parents could appreciate how much sense children talked, how wise they were. You could see it in the face of a newborn baby, that 'I know it all and you don't have to tell me' look.

'Who do you think really did it, Mrs Blake?'

'Did what, dearie?'

'Killed the bird-watcher.' Portia stared intently at Wilma.

'We'll know soon enough when the police work it out, dearie.'

'Will it be like that Agatha Christie play, when all the people in a hotel get killed off one by one?' Portia's tone is almost hopeful.

'Goodness, no! I expect it was just an accident.'

'I'm too young to die, Mrs Blake.' Portia looked down at her blue plastic swimming shoes.

What an odd thing for a child to say! 'Of course you are, dearie.' She put out a hand to touch the child. 'You mustn't fret yourself. These things happen sometimes. Mr Barrett was quite old. We all have to die one day.' She thought of her friend Barbara Scott's passion to book a corner of the Diddington graveyard. 'Some people have to die to make room for all the new ones being born.'

'Well, I know,' said Portia, 'except that it doesn't work quite like that, does it? I mean look at China, there's hundreds of millions of people there now, and there are going to be another nine hundred million or even more by the year 2000. It depends how much breeding there is, you see, Mrs Blake.' She made it sound like rabbits. 'I don't approve of breeding, Mrs Blake. What do you think?'

'Well, there's breeding and there's breeding, isn't there, Portia? Some of it's all right. We're all a result of breeding, you know.'

'I know.' The child wrinkled up her face. 'But it's disgusting, isn't it?'

Wilma laughed. She took a green phial out of her big black bag. 'Give these pills to your mother, dearie. Two, at most three, at night. They're nothing to do with breeding, but they should help with her pains.'

As Portia bore remedies to her mother, Crispin Delancey bore his family off for a bit of restorative culture. The orange sign outside Caunos said: 'Enterence Price One Person 10,000 T.L.' A Turk looked at them suspiciously from the window of a small Portakabin. Crispin paid and got out his guide. He was determined to do something properly. 'Caunos was the son of Miletus,' he announced. The girls looked bored instantly. 'His sister fell in love with him, and when he went away she hanged herself. Hence the expression "a Caunian love".'

'Never heard it,' said Dodo.

'No, well.' He ploughed on. 'The city was renowned for its unhealthy air. Caunians were sick a lot. They blamed it on the fruit, but it was actually the mosquitoes.' Dodo wondered whether they should be taking malaria tablets. But both the Proper Holiday's agent and the BA travel bureau had said it wasn't necessary. 'During the Roman Empire, Caunos did well, especially with slaves and salt. They made glue, too.'

Jade sniffed. 'And even now you can still smell it!'

'Can you?'

'Of course you can't. I wish you could.'

'Jade!'

'Over there,' said Crispin, waving, 'is the amphitheatre. Let's go and have a look.'

It was impressive, particularly when you considered how long it had been there, and through how many cultural upheavals, wars and revolutions. Thirty rows of stone seats were carved into the hillside, with ten stairways and two arched entrances on the northern side. But a lot of it was crumbling, and two olive trees had made their home in rows five and fourteen. Dodo climbed up to the top and sat down. She felt dizzy. Crispin sat down next to her.

'Can I have the water,' she said, 'please?' Crispin unhooked the rucksack from his back and peered inside. No water. 'You haven't forgotten it, have you?'

'I'm sorry.'

'Why is it,' she began, and he knew what'd be coming next,

'that you can't remember *anything ever*? You leave it all to me, don't you? You can't take any *responsibility*, can you? You just want the good side of family life without any of the work!'

A busload of German tourists invaded the amphitheatre, and several passed by what was clearly a marital argument in any language. Dodo moved away from Crispin in disgust, so there was a space between them. A small lizard darted into it, its pink tongue searching for tourist titbits.

Crispin apologized again. He hadn't meant to forget the water. He was sure they'd be able to buy some from the man in the Portakabin.

Down below, Jade pointed to Crispin and Dodo up on the top row and said to Star, 'What do you bet they're arguing again?'

'Do you think Mum knows?'

'No. Do you?'

Star shook her head. Dodo was horribly trusting. It was the same with them. Though she worried all the time, she was incapable of believing they would actually wilfully do anything bad. 'You're not going to say anything, are you? We're going home in a few days. It'll be all right then. Dad's not really like that. It's just a . . .'

'I know, it's just a phase he's going through,' echoed Jade. 'Hey listen, Star, I talked to Josh. He's got this plan to hire some bikes and take off for a trip into the hills. What d'you say?'

'I'll think about it.'

At the top of the amphitheatre, Dodo looked out beyond the ruined city to the marshlands either side of the river which flowed out to the sea. The sun made mirrors of water riddling the plains, bright mirrors in amongst the mud. Looking at all that water, it was even more difficult to forget her thirst. 'Oh Crispin, what's happening to us?'

Crispin looked down at the fruits of their loins kicking Roman stones around the floor of the amphitheatre, which must have been home to so many more noble events. 'Nothing. Nothing's happening. It's just the holidays. It'll be all right when we get home, you'll see.'

Dodo thought about the house in Tanza Road, about the cleanliness and comfort of it all – the white gloss paint in the kitchen, the new portable phone, the way her new Turkish rugs would look (when she'd told Crispin about them) on the old pine floors, the view out over the garden to the tops of the trees on the Heath. She thought about Bea Meredith next door with her sons and her lovers, and of Mr Ridgeway the other side, with his fine wistaria and habit of offering her cuttings of plants she'd already got. She thought of the rain, and the dog shit on the pavements, and the problems with the new residents' parking scheme.

'Yes, I suppose you're right.'

'I am right.' But was he looking forward to going home the way she was?

'Crispin, we haven't made love since the first night here.'

'Haven't we? Well, you were ill.'

'We usually do it every other night on holiday.'

'Do we?' It was amazing how women kept a mental record of these things. On the other hand, he'd known it was only a matter of time before she noticed.

'I'm sorry.'

'Like you are about the water?'

'No, not like I am about the water. Stop hounding me, Dodo.' He got up and walked away from her.

Crispin was hardly ever angry like this. Dodo was afraid. She climbed down, nearly missing her step several times, to look for the girls, but they seemed to have disappeared. A woman with a purple scarf tied over her hair and an earnest face was taking a group of tourists around. 'And on the external wall of the west façade of the fountain, you will find an inscription. This is the custom regulations for the boats that docked in the harbour. Please note the white flowering plant on the left. This is the styrax, which we find in only three places in the world.'

When they got back to the hotel, Carly Atkins was in reception. 'He had a heart attack,' she told them. 'Mr Barrett, that is. He wasn't a well man.'

'But what was he doing in the sulphur baths,' asked Dodo, 'all on his own?'

'That was what I said.'

'And why did he have a heart attack there?'

'Exactly.'

Crispin took his walkman and settled down by the pool to listen to 'Bridge over Troubled Water' again. While he was lying there more or less on his own (the honeymooners were opposite, but he didn't count them), Joshua Holbeach walked past, a rangy, bent figure against the still horribly blue-and-yellow sky. Joshua had a few days' teenage growth on his face, and his dark hair and his clothes were dirty. He looked as though he were looking for someone. 'Are you looking for someone?' asked Crispin, pulling the earphones out of his ears.

The young man shrugged, but stood there.

'I think your family's gone to Surlyu for the day.'

'Thanks.' He wandered off again. Dodo said Jade had fallen for Joshua. He could understand why. Joshua represented disorder, matter-out-of-place – all the things Dodo, despite her flower power beginnings, didn't want her daughters to do or be.

'Hey, man!' Crispin summoned Joshua back. 'You got any spare hash?'

Joshua's face crumbled into a grin. 'Sure. I didn't know you folks were into it. Well, not with me, but I can getcha some. Back in an hour or so.'

Crispin didn't know quite what had come over him, but it was as though some tight string had twanged inside him. The desire for disorder, for chaos, for the freedom to do and be nothing had taken hold of him.

It had proved to be a fairly disastrous day all round, what with his and Dodo's argument in Caunos, and then Kelly Upton got attacked by bees ('It was her fault for fiddling with the lids of those boxes,' said her mother nastily), Grizelda Dunkerley overdosed on Senokot and was back to where she started, and when the Holbeaches came back from their trip, Sandy found that her credit card was missing. 'You should have taken it with you, you silly bitch!' said husband Martin.

'But I hid it inside a Tampax box!' she cried. 'It ought to have been safe enough there.'

'Bleeding thief!' commented Martin.

About the same time as his father commented on the theft of his mother's credit card, their son observed that it was rush hour in the harbour by the Karput pizza bar. Joshua was watching the blue and white boats with their blue canvas roofs coming home for the night. A whole flotilla was at this very moment jostling to be arranged in the surprisingly unproblematic local double parking system. The boatmen of Karput had long ago formed themselves into a co-operative. This seemed to keep the prices stable, and prevented men outbidding one another. Contrary to their ethnic image, the Turks of the Dina-cek valley were interested in co-operation, not conflict.

Joshua had a glass of neat vodka at his elbow, and was waiting to meet Yusuf and Celik. Yusuf and Celik were themselves waiting for a new batch of hash-hash to arrive from a village upstream known for its fertile properties. They sat down next to him.

'The boat will arrive soon,' said Yusuf, looking at his new Swiss gold watch. 'How much you want?'

Joshua took a bundle of dirty lire from his back pocket and counted: 100,000: about £10. He put it away again. 'That's all I've got.' He was short on cash.

'Where the girls are, then?' asked Celik brightly.

'They'll be here at eight o'clock,' replied Joshua, pointing at his own Swatch digital watch. Jade and Star and Kelly, that is. Portia'd been recalled to base camp, thank God, the kid was really still in nappies. Star was hanging around Aaron now, goody-goody Aaron.

'When the girls come, where we go then?' asked Yusuf.

'I thought we might rent some bikes, go off somewhere. Problem is the dough, though.'

'Dough?'

'Money.'

'Ah, yes.'

'How much will it cost?'

Yusuf frowned. He had a friend in the local motorbike shop. 'Fifty thousand, maybe.'

'Do they take a credit card?'

'Excuse me?'

Joshua made a sign in the air. 'Visa card, American Express.'

'Oh, yes.'

'That's okay, then.' He withdrew the card from his back pocket, and flashed it around. 'This should do the trick. Oh, and we'll need another girl. One more girl.' He shouted to make his meaning clear. 'Think you can find one?'

Yusuf and Celik turned to each other and laughed. 'Maybe.'

'Good, good. Things are looking up around here!'

Just before eight, the three girls sauntered round the corner of the mosque. Jade was wearing a short-sleeved white lace affair over a black vest and a short flared skirt; she had a new collection of silver bangles and rings and chains, but her unlaced DMs were the same. Star hadn't dressed for the occasion, and wore her usual all-enveloping t-shirt. Kelly was in espadrilles and black lycra shorts with a tight white top. Her olive skin was deep brown now, and her short boyish hair was streaked pale with the sunlight and a bottle of peroxide. Joshua ordered more vodka. 'Have you girls eaten yet?' he asked expansively.

'No, we got off supper by claiming we wanted to see the last turtle video before the place closes for the night. That Holbeach woman went, and she's raving about it.'

'And they believed you?'

'Not so much believed as had other things to think about,' observed Jade realistically. 'The travel rep's there again. That bird-watching dude, they say he died from natural causes, but nobody believes it. And apparently your mother's had her credit card stolen.' She looked at Joshua quizzically. 'Aaron said he'd be coming later.'

'News from home, eh? No wonder I avoid the place. Have some food then?'

'We haven't got any money.'

'I have. This evening's on me.'

'Well, that's very nice of you, Joshua,' said Jade, remembering her manners. 'I'll have a three-cheese pizza with absolutely masses of anchovies.'

'I'll have the same but with onions,' said Kelly.

'Chips'll do me,' said Star.

'Doncha ever eat?' He eyed her skinniness with disapproval. 'The Turks like their women fat, don't they, Yusuf!'

Star wriggled on the seat. 'Doesn't matter what I eat, I can do without food, you know. Doesn't mean I'm anorexic, though. But that's what my mum keeps going on about.'

'I know, I know. Oh by the way, I ordered an extra girl, just in case.'

Celik returned towing a large female in a green and pink elastic dress with high white sandals and blonde dark-rooted hair. 'Pleased to meet Tansil,' he explained. 'She work in a shop.' Tansil giggled and sat down on Celik's knee.

'I have fixed the bikes,' he said turning to Joshua. 'But where we go on them?'

'Hows about Galata?' Joshua named a small town he'd read about that seemed the nearest thing to the industrial West you could find in these parts. It had chrome mines and a paper mill, and therefore other things as well, he assumed.

Yusuf and Celik nodded. 'Palkan is more beautiful.'

'We're not out for the beauty, chaps, we're out for the night life, aren't we, girls?'

In the end they agreed to go to Galata, a forty-kilometre or so trip, but passing Palkan on the way there or back. Aaron arrived just as they were loading themselves on to the bikes. He took one of them. 'I'm really glad to see you,' whispered Star.

'Is this your idea of revenge?'

'Well, something like it. Yes. I suppose so.'

As the sun dropped behind the mountain, and the masts of the boats jangled in the evening breeze, the little convoy left Karput by the north-east road up into the mountains, and then down again into the valley. Yusuf and Kelly went first; Star and Aaron followed, then Celik and Tansil, with Jade and Joshua coming last. Jade wrapped her arms tightly round Joshua's lean body. She could feel his ribs under the thin white t-shirt. She was light-headed from the vodka. As Joshua got his measure of the bike, and accelerated up the bleached stone-ridden mountain road, Jade felt the cooler air rush through her long multi-coloured hair and draw it out behind her and enter all the crevices of her clothes, so that her whole body was floating on air. An extra buzz was provided by the fact that no one knew where they were or where they were going. She was glad to be getting away from the whole steamy mess.

That night, unaware of what his daughters are doing, Crispin knows what he has to do, but, before doing it, he takes himself off for a walk by the river and rolls himself a nice little cigarette to give himself some Dutch courage. It brings back the days of his youth; the pre-Jade and Star days, when no one used the word 'responsibility' accusingly at him. Up above, the diamond stars twinkle knowingly, and he takes a yellow rose and crushes its petals in his hands to take the smell of the hash away. He brushes his teeth well before getting into bed. Dodo is reading a book about turtles. He reaches out for her.

'You don't have to do it just because I complained you hadn't,' she observes double-bindingly. But he does do it, just. Afterwards she cries. 'Hold me, Crispin!' she beseeches, but as that's what he's doing anyway, it's not a problem.

TEN

Jade's Dream

The other side of the mountains from Karput, day breaks with an explosion of light through the trees of the forest outside the town where the young people have settled down for what remains of the night. Yusuf and Celik have brought sleeping bags and rugs. When the light bursts between the trees, as though someone has trained an immense electric lamp on her face, Jade sits up, startled, rubbing her eyes. They feel as though they have sand in them. Her head hurts, and there's a nasty stale taste in her mouth. Her hair is tangled, and when she runs her hand through it, she finds bits of sticks and leaves in it. Quietly, so as not to wake the others, she get out of the Turkish sleeping bag and pads through the trees to a clearing which looks down on to a stream. In the crisp morning light the stream runs like diamonds over yellow stones. Following it further down the incline of the hillside, she comes to a small pool, where a dip in the earth stops and holds the water for a while, before allowing it to trickle on down the hill to feed the industry of the sour-faced chrome mills on the outskirts of Galata.

Jade stops by the edge of the pool, and looks down into it. The diamond water and the sunlight look back at her, and mixed with their glances is the image of her own upside-down head, with its gritty eyes and knotted black and purple hair.

She bends and dips her hands in the pool, and puts the clear cold water on her face, and that makes her feel better, and she takes off her socks, which are wet anyway, from her walk through the dew of the forest floor, and puts one foot and then the other in, and that is cold, but it seems to do something for her headache, which is shocked into leaving her by the sudden sensation of coldness at both ends of her body.

They'd reached Galata about eleven last night. Because Joshua had persuaded someone to give him some cash on his mother's credit card, knowing the card would soon be stopped, if it hadn't been already, there'd been quite a lot of money, and unlimited access to drinks. Jade had started with rum-and-Cokes, but after the fourth she'd begun to feel nauseous. Star had only had one. Kelly had gone on putting them down. It was quite amazing how much that girl could get through without any ill effects. Kelly was like a bright tin nail – hard through and through. She'd told Jade that she was on the pill at fourteen, and that she'd first made love with a boy when she was thirteen, in the park opposite her school, on the way home one summer Thursday evening. It was a quick fuck, as Kelly put it: their first and last. Since then there'd been others, equally quick. 'There's nothing to it, you take it from me,' said Kelly knowingly. 'It's absolutely nothing to make a fuss about. The sooner you find that out the better.'

Both Kelly and Jade want to make love with Joshua. Joshua exudes sex along with the grime and the sweat that lines his clothes. He radiates trapped physical energy, the movements of his body promise accomplished conjugation. Like Kelly, Joshua makes no secret of the record of his bodily experiences, mostly achieved in his case in the copses of Hampstead Heath, which offer a sanctuary to many fuckers and lovers, though it's as well to know the times of the circuits of the park police, who have a habit of shining bright torches on the pale faces and interlocked bodies of those who don't, just as the Turkish sun had managed to find Jade and her friends, by searching through the gaps in the aromatic pine trees and penetrating these with a sharp interrogatory light.

The scent in the forest reminds Jade of the Sainsbury's disinfectant Dodo uses in the lavatories in Tanza Road. The conjunction of the two scents is weird: the one domestic, reeking of the still-needed security of home and family; the other beckoning her on to a vast unknown realm of exciting independent delights. Joshua says they have enough money to last until after the end of the holiday – he wants them to stay on the road, as he puts it, until after the plane bearing all their troubled parents safely back home will have taken off from the soldiered zone of Karaman airport. Thoughtfully, unusually thoughtfully, perhaps inspired by the dancing ruminations of the sun through the forest and on the water, Jade considers the pros and cons of Joshua's plan. Joshua's in trouble one way or another. He's in trouble anyway with his parents. Jade isn't normally thankful for her own, when she looks at other people's, but she is in Joshua's case. Who would want a mother like Sandy, fussy, over-protective, and over-occupied with adopted babies, plucked according to no doubt dubious principles from their proper homes in faraway places and transplanted without any choice in the matter to the clay-logged site of Nassington Road? Joshua doesn't need a mother who's given up on him and started on someone else. The point is that you need your mother there in the background to rail against. If she's not there, your railing has no focus, and can get out of hand. Sitting by the pool in the pine forest, smelling the odours of Dodo's cleaning materials all about her, Jade feels suddenly such an unexpected rush of love for Dodo: the vision of the perfect mother, perfect in her absence precisely because not present, appears before her, hung in the glittering space between two trees the other side of the mirror pool of golden water. The lady who is Dodo in form with Dodo's oh-so-familiar face wears a gown of blue, but also rubber gloves, and holds a green bottle of disinfectant. She hovers there for a moment, making suggestive cleansing and beckoning motions, among the early dragonflies and other forest insects, and with the sun forming a crisp frill of sacred brilliance around her, and then is gone just as suddenly, moving off to do her housework elsewhere.

Jade rubs her eyes. Her own unaccompanied face looks back at her from the pool. It must be the rum. She moves her feet among the grassy rocks at the edge of the water. In which something moves, and she stares; out of what must seem to it like a rainforest ambles a grey-brown tortoise, old as the ruins Jade won't take seriously when her father reads to her from guidebooks about them, with its plated house on its back and its crinkly leathery limbs hardly distinguishable from the rocks and the stones. It ambles out and stands in front of her, and fixed her with two yellow eyes in a head that reminds her of the extra-terrestrial creature that had been a media hit in the mid-1980s, when her father had bought her and Star two furry versions from Hamley's. The tortoise's eyes are unblinking. It's a curiously still, knowing regard. The tortoise is wise because it's very, very old. No, not because it's old, for if wisdom comes only with age, how is it some adults are so silly? Jade speaks to the tortoise in a low voice, so as not to startle the forest. 'Hallo, old chap. Is this your home, here? Do you come out every morning like this, when the sun lights the forest, do you come out of the grass just to see what can be seen, and to stare at it? Look at me, I'm a runaway teenager. I'm wild, I'm a problem to my parents. You understand that, don't you? I expect you've had a whole army of little ones in your time. What did you do about it when they stayed out all night? I expect you just looked at them like you're looking at me now, didn't you?'

Jade remembers with a pang like the sharp breaking of twigs in a forest as an animal steps over them her father's alliance with the golden-headed Meg Shaw. So far as she knows, he's never done anything like that before. That's one reason why it's so shocking. The other shocking thing is that while Dodo is there, physically, she seems not to have noticed, but she must be the only person in the Hotel Rhapsody Palas who hasn't. Do all men have midlife crises? Is Joshua's father having one, too? Is that why he's so rude to everyone, banging his fist on the table when they don't agree with him? Is that why he'd said he was going back to England, when all he did was put on women's clothes and check into the Goy Motel?

Jade had told Joshua about his father. Joshua had whistled: 'Well whadda you know!' But he hadn't, and Jade could tell it shocked him. The ways of fathers are as dubious as the ways of mothers. Jade knows that Star has talked to Aaron about the relationship between her father and his mother. Perhaps their uncountenanced absence here in Galata will bring the whole lot of them to their senses. It's not so much that Jade wants to keep her mother and father together, in some sort of cosy family formula, it's that she doesn't want to be bothered with having to think about what they're up to, when she and her sister are the ones who should be up to things. Dodo and Crispin have had their own time; Mr and Mrs Delancey had their chance before they became Mr and Mrs Delancey, and now it's the next generation's turn.

Behind Jade, the rest of the forest stirs and wakes up, including Joshua, who stumbles down through the trees to find her by the pool. 'Jesus, I'm thirsty! Have we got any juice?' Does he expect a fridge full of freshly squeezed orange juice? She points at the pool. 'You think it's okay to drink?'

She shrugs. 'God knows.'

Joshua strips off his t-shirt and kneels over the pool and splashes water over his face and thin brown body, and then drinks some, cupping it inefficiently in his hands.

'You wouldn't be much good at survival, would you?' she comments. 'I bet you couldn't even light a forest fire.'

He brings a cigarette lighter out of the back pocket of his jeans. 'That I could.'

She laughs. Stuck to the cigarette lighter is the credit card. It falls into the grass, its laser wings flashing.

'There was a tortoise here earlier.'

'How fucking interesting.'

'It looked at me.'

'You probably gave it a heart attack, like the old bird-watcher.'

'I think we should go back, Josh.'

'Well, I don't. It's just beginning to be fun. Let's take a bike and go down into the town and find some food. One hour, one day at a time, babe. Who knows what the day will bring? The world's our playpen. Why, from where we are we can't ever see the bars!' He leans over and kisses her roughly; she feels the wetness of his body and the scratchy surface of his face on hers, and smells the residue of last night's pizza, mixed with the raw vodka he'd been drinking. 'You don't know what I got last night,' he boasts.

'What?'

'These.' From inside the waist of his jeans he brings out a rumpled squeeze of toilet paper, and shows her a few tiny white pills. 'Es. We can take them tonight. You ever had an E?'

'Yes,' she lies.

'They're no big deal, are they, but man, they give you a fierce trip!'

When the others have woken up, they all get on their bikes and go down into Galata and find a café and have eggs and bread and honey and hot sweet coffee. Afterwards, Star wants to brush her teeth. 'How fucking bourgeois!'

'I don't care. I'm going to buy a toothbrush.'

'We might just wait for you,' says Josh off-handedly. They watch her as she walks across the square, goes into a pharmacy, and comes out with a red toothbrush and a tube of Colgate.

By the time she comes back, they've hatched a plan. 'We're going north to Knodrum,' they say. 'It's a big town, it'll have more of a night life.' Aaron looks at Star as if to say it's okay, don't worry, I'll look after us, it's all under control.

The bikes are burning when they get back on to them. Jade makes sure she gets on behind Josh before Kelly has a chance to. Once they've picked up some speed, things cool down. Jade presses her arms round Josh's ribs. Man, that feels good. Her legs kneadle the back pocket of his jeans. On one side is the cigarette lighter, the credit card and a wad of lire. Out of the other pocket sticks a notebook. He writes in it from time to time. 'What d'you write in that?' she'd asked him a few days ago.

'Notes. It's a notebook.'

'For what, though?'

'None of your fucking business.'

They reach Knodrum as the sun is almost on top of the sky. The road becomes dustier, and litter appears at its edges as they pass the usual shabby buildings that line the approaches to the town. They see a police car once, but it crosses the road in front of them and then disappears. Jade's headache is back again. 'We'll take some rooms in a pansiyon tonight,' says Josh. 'One night under the stars is enough for me. I don't want no animals coming and looking at me in my sleep.'

The woman in the Pansiyon Biddeka is only faintly curious. Josh gives her a bundle of notes. They take three rooms. Josh takes Jade's bag with the bundle from his bike and dumps them both on the narrow bed of the largest room, the only one with a balcony. The balcony looks over the main street. 'Those who pay get the best,' he says. 'I'm going to take a shower before we hit the town.'

There's a bit of a fight about the other two rooms. Kelly doesn't want to share with the other girls, but they do: Tansil, for all her come-hither gestures, is a good Moslem girl, and Star, as she'd told Wilma Blake back in the Rhapsody Palas, is definitely not into sex. Kelly is basically peeved about not getting Josh to herself, but there's nothing any of them can do about that.

Jade lies down on the bed in the big room. The glare from the window is like the sun through the trees of the forest. She gets up and pulls the thin grey-and-orange-striped curtain across it, and lies down again. She can hear Yusuf and Celik in the next room – they seem to be moving furniture around. Down the corridor, Joshua splashes in the shower. The late night and the early rising catch up with her, and in a minute she's asleep.

She has the queerest dream. She and Star are at school, but

instead of being taught, they're teachers. They stand in front of the class, but next to two gleaming Turkish motorbikes. They have cropped hair, both of them, and they wear Victorian dresses with lace collars. Star points to some letters in a strange script on the board. 'It's all Greek to me,' says a student in the front row – Martin Holbeach, with his mascara-ed eyes and baggy Turkish costume. He leans back and wraps his face in his silk scarf with a defiant, bored, 'I've had enough of this' gesture.

In the corner of the room, Sandy Holbeach is being sick and Lisa Upton is methodically scooping up the vomit and storing it under the floorboards. 'You shouldn't do that,' says Portia, standing there in her demure tartan frock. 'It's rude.'

Lisa pulls at her silver cross. 'Don't you lecture me, young lady. I know about God. He lives in Chigwell, just round the corner from us. But he goes to Venice for his holidays *and* he's joined BUPA.'

'But does he know who killed the bird-watcher?' asks Portia.

'I thought you weren't talking to me!'

'Shush!' says Star from the podium. 'Be quiet, girls, you can talk about what's happening on *Neighbours* after class, not in it.'

'Of course God knows,' says Lisa. 'God knows everything. That's why he's in BUPA. It was a self-inflicted death. Mr Barrett worked with the dead, didn't he? Well, you can't expect to be working class and get away with it for ever, you know.'

Next to Lisa is Eileen Barrett, sobbing and holding her head in her hands. 'Take these,' instructs Wilma Blake, scooping a handful of pills out of a handbag the size of a dustbin. 'They're no big deal, are they, but man, they give you a fierce trip!' She cackles. 'I know just how you're feeling, dearie. Indeed, I know much more than any of you think I do.'

'She does, she does!' Ronald Dunkerley is hovering above the desks like an apparition. 'And I am a professor, I see and understand everything.'

Below him, Crispin Delancey and Derrick Upton hoot with laughter. 'No smoking in class, please,' says Star firmly. 'The inspectors will be round soon.'

Crispin and Derrick are wreathed in hash smoke, from behind which their peals of laughter shoot out across the ghostly vomit-strewn classroom. 'That chap up there,' Crispin is doubled up with laughter, 'that chap only knows about the past. But the past doesn't work any more, you see, that's the problem! Isn't it, Derrick? You're an energy consultant, you ought to know!'

'Yes, I've got the energy to know, haven't I?' Derrick collapses in gales of laughter, too.

A coffin glides into the room. It has the little yellow eyes of a tortoise. The lid springs open and Kizi Demir sits up in a smart black suit with a waiter's bow tie. He speaks with a mechanical voice, like the one used by Stephen Hawking, author of *A Brief History of Time*. 'There's too much spying going on round here, far too much. I won't have it in my hotel.' The lid closes again, and the coffin reverses out of the doorway.

'I don't know what he means, dear, but have you made your bed and taken your vitamin pills?' Dodo, at the back of the room, has put up her hand to speak. 'Oh, and I've just seen to Miss Shaw. I pushed her into the sulphur baths. She smells revolting. Aaron can come and live with us, he won't be any trouble. He can watch the show with the rest of us.' She points to the front of the room, where the two Joans are dancing arm-in-arm like Folies Bergères girls, but stripped entirely naked, except for their red nail polish. 'Ta-ra-ra boom-de-ay,' they sing, and their white flesh bounces up and down, and they go on and on enjoying themselves, oblivious of the appalled silence that has fallen over all the other characters in the room.

ELEVEN

The Maid's Story

Away from the pine forests of Galata, and the disturbed dreams of disturbed adolescents, it was scorchingly hot in Karput, and especially in the Hotel Rhapsody Palas. There'd been no rain since the storm that night when the youth club went to Turtle Beach and Ronald Dunkerley skinny-dipped with Sandy Holbeach. No clouds had been seen in the infinite reaches of the sapphire sky, and only the globes and discs and twinkles of the heavenly bodies broke up its monotonous blueness by shining inquiringly down on the doings of those, especially those in the Hotel Rhapsody Palas, who could have done with a good deal more illumination than they had.

Carly Atkins was standing in reception. 'What do you mean, they've disappeared?'

Mehmet Lorca moved paperwork around the desk with an attitude of suppressed irritation. 'They have gone, all of them, somewhere without saying where it is they are going. Of course, they could have been kidnapped, but that is unlikely as Yusuf and Celik Medrese are with them, also a girl from the Medrese family too, a cousin, I think.'

Carly puffed and swore and shifted her weight from one high-heeled sandal to another. She'd just about managed to capture Matt the other night, but the battle wasn't over yet. Also, she wasn't feeling very well, and it wasn't her throat this time.

'The police have been called.'

They had, and Detective Denzli Jarmu was soon back at the Hotel Rhapsody Palas suffering from equally suppressed irritation. 'What kind of establishment are you running here, Mehmet? Don't you think we have better things to do, especially at this time of year, and now the military police are short-staffed?'

Mehmet apologized. But his hotel was full of overwrought parents. Dodo, particularly. She'd had a hot and tiring day on the minibus to and from the market at Kitayuk, where she'd bought a roll of Osborne and Little curtain fabric only to find when she got it home that it had a big grey line down the middle. There'd been a note on Jade's pillow the following morning. 'DON'T WORRY WE KNOW WHAT WE'RE DOING' it said.

'This is not much help, is it, Mrs Dee-lan-zee?' said Denzli Jarmu when she gave it to him. 'They know, but we don't. But never despair, we will find your daughters for you!'

Dodo's imagination was working overtime. 'But supposing there's a murderer around here? Suppose someone killed poor Mr Barrett, and now they're after our children! Perhaps it's the Kurds!'

Crispin thought of renting a car and driving out of Karput to look for them, but that probably wouldn't help much either.

'I wish he'd never been born!' said Sandy Holbeach of her son, Joshua.

Little Primrose held her adoptive mother's skirts nervously, and little thin-bodied Freddie would have sucked both thumbs if he could have done. Sandy was shocked to hear herself say this, and husband Martin was shocked, too. 'Come on, old Josh isn't *that* bad!'

'It's not what he's doing – I'm used to that. It's the others – the other parents, they're all blaming him and so they're blaming me, and I've had enough of it!'

'Well, you can understand it, though, can't you?' he said, appealing, he thought, to her professional side.

'I'm tired of understanding people,' declared Sandy. 'I think I'd rather just hate them.'

'Suit yourself.'

'What about the Turkish lads?' asked Derrick Upton. 'Don't they have parents who'd know where they are? What about the local girl? Can't we find them that way?'

'Mr Upton,' said Denzli Jarmu, after having done some of the detective work for which he was paid, 'Yusuf and Celik's parents thought they were in Karput. Tansil's mother – her father can't be traced – says she has enough to do with her five younger brothers and sisters without worrying about what nightclubs her daughter might be in. We shall just have to wait for news. But I'm perfectly sure that there's no criminal element here. We must only hope that they return before Saturday. I understand the aeroplane will take you back to London then.'

'Stansted, actually.'

'Ah yes.' Gareth Barrett, or rather Gareth Barrett's body, should be on the plane, too, that is, provided the paperwork could be completed in time, and provided they could find a large enough refrigerated van to take him in – Gareth Barrett was, and still is, a big man.

Denzli had also managed to track down the source of the bikes the young people had hired – a shop between the mosque and the Post Office specializing in the rental of small industrial and agricultural machines. The owner of the pizza bar had reported the assembly of young people and bikes, and had given good descriptions of all of them, even naming Tansil, whom he knew slightly, as her mother ran the carpet shop that had poisoned Dodo Delancey and Grizelda Dunkerley.

The business of the stolen credit card was a lot easier. Denzli knew the staff of the hotel well – they were honest, and anyway it wouldn't be in their interests to steal from their clients. It seemed pretty clear that the Holbeach boy had taken his mother's card. After much debating, he'd disclosed his suspicion to both Mr and Mrs Holbeach. Their reactions had surprised him. 'I told her she'd hid it in a stupid place,' was all Mr Holbeach said. 'I don't suppose it'll be the last time, either,' said Mrs Holbeach.

'So you see,' explained Denzli to Mehmet Lorca and Carly Atkins, 'it is all a bit of a mess. It is your bad luck, Mehmet, for having decided to go into the tourist business. Most people find the Germans easier. I think it is because they do not have as much imagination.' He laughed and hit Mehmet encouragingly on the back.

Bilge Hassoun brought them a tray of apple tea. The other staff were excited by all these events, but Bilge felt weary. She was tired, and the lentil crop had failed, and Gultas had said they couldn't afford their day out in Ocakkoy. All these happenings in the hotel seemed to her a huge fuss about nothing. Or, rather, about something that could be avoided: the uncontrolled behaviour of young people. 'They come from a different culture,' Kizi had explained to her many times, but she never found this a satisfactory explanation. 'But they are all so unhappy,' she pointed out. 'The parents are unhappy – they look at their children and they worry – the children look at their parents and they hate them, and then the children and the parents, they both do things to make themselves forget all this. All this freedom, it is not good, Kizi.'

It was in the *Daily Mail*, too. 'MYSTERY OF DISAPPEARING TEENAGERS ON PARADISE HOLIDAY', it said, going on to suggest that either rings of drugs or spies must be involved. Jade was called Jayne, which upset Dodo unreasonably. Lisa Upton got her way with Derrick's nomenclature as an energy consultant, and old Josh appeared as the son of a communist writer, which Martin Holbeach couldn't have cared less about. It was rumoured that the recent death of Mr Gareth Barrett, a retired bank clerk, in the local mud (not sulphur) baths might be connected with whatever ring had lured the teenagers away. The local rep from the travel company, Miss Caroline Adkings, was not available for comment, as she had been poisoned. Her mother was interviewed, making a couple of sour remarks about holidays in romantic places usually being worse than Scarborough on a bank holiday weekend. She was pictured with Carly's cat, a sulky flea-ridden castrate called Major, along-side one of Jayne and one of the Holbeaches en famille, looking studiously happy, and one of the Hotel Rhapsody Palas still being built and spelled 'PALACE'.

Wilma Blake, whose *Daily Mail* it was, read it quietly in her room when they'd all finished with it. It was far too hot for her outside. She looked at the photographs of Jade and of the Holbeach children. She looked out of her window to the poolside, where she could see Sandy Holbeach and Dodo Delancey sitting under umbrellas with cooling drinks, and her Derrick in the pool with Stevie and with Crispin Delancey. The men had a ball and had got some kind of game going, which involved trying to keep the ball out of the water. Little

Stevie was getting over-excited. Derrick was wearing his silly hat, but despite that he cut a good figure, brown and muscular, with the hair of an ape nesting the gold chain on his chest. Lisa was nowhere to be seen: she was probably lying down or on the phone to her mother back home listening to recriminations of Carly Atkins's mother's kind about the insanity of foreign holidays.

In the hotel reception, Denzli Jarmu got up to go. Carly Atkins stood up at the same time, but then immediately keeled over onto the marble floor with a shriek of pain.

Mehmet bent down: Carly was a dreadful white colour. Denzli listened to Carly's heart, but there was nothing wrong there, at least not physiologically. He would have loosened her blouse, but it was loose enough already. It was then that they all noticed a horrible red stain creeping all over the blue and white floor. 'I think you'd better call another ambulance, Mehmet,' said Denzli.

They waited while the ambulance came and Carly, who suddenly seemed rather like one of the errant teenagers, was lifted on to a stretcher and borne away. Mehmet telephoned Iris, the Proper Holidays rep in Surlyu. Iris would make the necessary medical arrangements, and would notify head office. She would make sure Carly was visited in hospital if that turned out to be necessary, and also that another rep would be available to take charge of the clientele in the Hotel Rhapsody Palas. 'This is important,' stressed Mehmet, 'as we have been having a few problems here.'

'I know,' said Iris. 'Carly told me.' What she'd actually said was that she was fed up with the whole bloody lot of them. She was thinking of chucking the whole thing in and going back to Scarborough to retrain as a computer consultant.

Bilge Hassoun watched the ambulance leave the hotel fore-court. She fetched a bucket of water and a mop to remove the blood from the floor. Then she took the tray of tea back to the kitchen. In the kitchen she stood feeling very hot and panicky, as though something terrible was about to happen to her. She felt like one of those volcanoes she'd seen pictures of, holding all that blood-red lava in, like Carly Atkins's blood, until it boiled so much it simply had to come out.

Kizi saw her standing there. 'Why don't you sit down for a bit, Bilge? You deserve a break.' Kizi was always so kind and considerate. She sat down and watched the cook mincing pink lamb for lunch. Boiling tears came to her eyes. Then she got up and went outside to the archway which led to the blue swimming pool under the hot yellow sun. The grass had been watered by Suleyman that morning. They could have done with some of that water the other side of the river; if they'd had it, the lentils might have been all right, and then Gultas would have been happy, and so would she, and there would have been money to save for her nephews' schooling in Marmaris, to get them the kind of Moslem education that really would equip them to be citizens of the world, rather than, as for these spoilt people, simply playthings in it.

On the deckchairs lay the Uptons and the Delanceys, and one of the Holbeaches and one of the Dunkerleys and Ms golden bikini Meg Shaw, all with their sun lotions and their travel guides and their sunglasses, their cameras, their little personal stereos, their paperbacks and their thick terry towels, and their drinks in special poolside glasses. Bilge stood there looking at them. Derrick Upton, getting out of the pool, saw her standing there, and was puzzled, and watched her for a minute, and then said something to one of the others, and then various faces in the deckchairs turned round and looked at her, wearing expressions of no more than a passing interest in the spectre of a Turkish maid watching them with her black eyes from the fringes of their luxury play space.

Bilge advanced towards them, and positioned herself behind the chairs in which Sandy Holbeach and Dodo Delancey were sitting. A heat haze lay over all of them, a net of golden light like amber. 'You're sick, all of you!' she shouted at them in Turkish through the golden light over the artificial blue pool, amid the aromas of perfumed sunblocks and other silly unguents. 'You're sick and stupid and selfish. You don't deserve your children, no wonder they've run away from you! You're none of you fit to be parents! You should be ashamed of yourselves.' There were tears in her eyes, and the red of her hotel uniform ran with sweat. She felt full of heat and feeling and tiredness, and she wanted to go on shouting at them and hurting them until they all came to their senses and understood what she was trying to tell them.

They all stared at her. Kizi came out of the kitchen where he'd been getting a new stock of ice, and Mehmet, the manager, came, and the two of them stood either side of her and grasped her arms tightly and led her away to Mehmet's private sitting room, where they laid her down on the couch and talked quietly above her head. She was crying like a volcano now. The more she cried, the more she remembered what it had felt like then.

It had been a hot day like this one, and she'd been going about her work in the hotel as usual. Little Manya, who was four, had been with her grandmother the other side of the river in the rickety farmhouse. The old woman had been bottling apricots for winter that day. Bilge had told Manya to help her grandmother. Manya hadn't been able to take her big brown eyes off the sticky mess of apricots on the big wooden table, and already by the time Bilge had left several had been diverted into Manya's hungry little mouth.

About eleven o'clock, the old grandmother who rowed tourists across the river had come to get her. 'There's been an accident, Bilge. Your Manya has been run over by a big tourist car.'

Bilge will never forget that moment. Everything stopped, it seemed that her own heart should as well. The hotel had been full of noise, but a frozen silence had hung between her and the old boat lady. Bilge was paralysed, she couldn't move and she couldn't speak.

Medicine in southern Turkey was even less sophisticated five years ago than it is now. Gultas had taken Manya on his tractor to the white clinic where Bilge had given birth to her. When Bilge got there, Manya had canvas screens round her bed. She had a great big bandage on her head, and the doctor said her legs were broken too. She was asleep. 'She is not asleep,' the doctor had explained kindly. 'She has had a big bang on her head, and there is probably bleeding inside. She is in a coma.' The doctor told her that Manya might not live, and if she did, it wouldn't be much of a life. She died at four o'clock in the afternoon. Bilge had sat for a long time with her dead daughter, and she knew there was a place beyond grief, a place where, even if you doubted it the rest of the time, you knew exactly what life meant and what an inestimable gift it is – a gift to be used well, to be wondered at, to be treasured, to be looked after – like Manya herself. For all their poverty, and for all the narrowness of their lives, no child could have been more loved and treasured than Manya. She was a child without malice, with a sweet urge of kindness in her, though not without naughtiness. A child without naughtiness would be like a rose without thorns. But Manya, for all her preciousness to them, was an ordinary child. It was in her very ordinariness that they were blessed.

The nurses had been very good. They'd come to check on her behind the canvas screens every now and then, and to bring her tea. Once the doctor had come back and had sat down beside her and had taken her hand and had asked her a few questions. A child's death could drive a mother mad. But what Bilge was doing was just being with her daughter for the last time. She'd wanted just to sit there and have the wonderful, ordinary feeling of being in the same place as her child – that feeling of which there is normally no consciousness, as it's the most taken-for-granted thing in the world.

When Bilge had taken her leave of Manya at last, she had wanted to uncover the whole of her little body and touch and kiss every bit of it. She'd seen this in the wild: in the nosing and petting and worrying of a stillborn lamb by a sheep, even in the desperate rasping of a mother cat's tongue over the body of a kitten. It was as though enough licking and kissing and moving will bring the body back to life. A mother's touch could mend limbs, infuse air into sagging lungs, and start thick red blood beating round veins again. A mother's love and only that!

It was Wilma Blake who had explained it all to them. 'Bilge had a child who died a few years ago. It was her only child. That's a big burden to carry round all the time. She was shouting at you all because she thinks you should be grateful to have your children. She thinks you don't understand what a gift children are. I expect the heat had got to her, too, and then her husband's farm isn't doing very well, either.'

'How do you know all this, Mother?' The water on Derrick's bronzed body was evaporating before Wilma's eyes.

'I talked to Kizi. By the way, he said the manager would like us to accept his apologies. Nothing like this will ever happen again.'

'Well, I bloody well hope not,' said Martin Holbeach.

'Mind you,' said Wilma, gripping her handbag, 'I've got some sympathy with Bilge's point of view.'

'Mother!'

'Well, look at you all. You're a dissolute lot, aren't you! No wonder your youngsters ran away from you!'

Ronald Dunkerley stepped out of the shadows. 'I know who you are, don't I? You used to work in intelligence, didn't you? We met in a church, the Church of St Mary the Virgin in Bottesford, by the north transept. Very fine example of a man's head with a double serpent, one head biting his eye and the other his tongue.'

'The liar who loses sight of the truth and the power to speak it,' said Wilma Blake quietly. 'Yes, you're right, Professor Dunkerley, we did. That's *my* secret life – or was. And it was a darn sight more worthwhile than the one some of you are leading now!'

This time the Uptons were so shaken they couldn't utter the expletive 'Mother!' any more.

Wilma Blake sat down in the shade, and Ronald Dunkerley moved another chair over to sit beside her. 'Well, don't all look at us with open mouths, haven't you got some holidaying to get on with?' The witch-like laughter was the same, but Wilma's accent seemed more refined now.

'Gosh!' said Portia Dunkerley finally. 'Gosh! Did you really, Daddy? What sort of intelligence was that?'

'It's what enables one to understand things, dear. But I've always been better at the past than the present, as you know. Go on, Mrs Blake, haven't you got something to say? You've been watching everything. You understand, don't you?'

'I do, I do,' she said, 'but do all of *you* really want to? Does the point of life lie in understanding, or does it lie in just being able to carry on? Mr Barrett had AIDS, that's why he was in the sulphur baths, he thought it might cure him. But he had a heart attack because Mr Holbeach came in dressed as a woman, when he was supposed to be in Whitechapel, and Mr Holbeach had to try to make Mr Barrett promise not to tell. But dressing as a woman isn't a crime, or the prisons'd be full of us!'

Sandy turned to her husband in amazement. 'Is this true, Martin?'

He sighed deeply and then gasped for air. 'Can we talk about it later?'

'You should have talked about it before,' admonished Wilma Blake. 'So should Mr Barrett and his wife. And as for you, son,' she turned to Derrick, 'it's time you stopped finding other ways of getting money to buy your pretty little Lisa things she doesn't need. You're lucky the police aren't on to you as well as the Holbeach boy, but then there's so much drug-dealing round here and the local economy so depends on it that they do have to turn something of a blind eye.'

Before Lisa could ask her husband if this was true, Ronald took over. 'And the women aren't blameless, are they, Mrs Blake? There are enough alcoholics and anorexics here to fill a hospital ward!' He leant back in his chair and laughed. Mrs Blake joined in. And then they all did, one by one, in a fit of collective hysteria, which is how Mehmet found them when he came out to tell them that Aaron Shaw had called from the post office in Galata to say they'd all be back in the morning.

TWELVE

Fly and Smile

Later that day, the two Joans went in the hotel minibus to visit Carly Atkins in the hospital in Ocakkoy. Carly was in a ward with lots of other people with miscellaneous complaints, from dislocated shoulders and duodenal ulcers to prolapsed recta, collapsed lungs, and broken hearts. Carly's trouble turned out to have been given her by the ex-geography teacher – a baby. However, he gave it to her in the wrong place. The baby had been growing in one of her fallopian tubes, which had burst, expelling three pints of blood into her abdomen and causing her to faint with pain and shock. Since Carly hadn't even known she was pregnant, the whole thing was even more of a shock than it was when she fainted. 'The bastard!' she kept saying. 'I'll get him for this!' In between swearing, she cried and wanted her mum back in Scarborough, which the nurses, who were all Turkish and had limited English, understood better.

Carly lay there with a new scar on the outside of her abdomen, and tears on her face, and the dark roots of her bleached hair showing, and having recriminatory fantasies about the ex-geography teacher, and also about the bosomy Hilda, whom in some obscure way she blamed for all of this, and the two Joans arrived, bearing grapes, and a selection of reading matter from the hotel, including Nicholas Salaman's *Falling Apart* and a book called *Reliving Past Lives*, which contained Startling New Evidence of Reincarnation, and which they thought might cheer Carly up.

As usual, Carly didn't recognize them at first – the hotels she looked after were full of women who looked like them. But then, when they began talking, and mentioned words like 'drugs' and 'bird-watching' and 'credit card', it came back to her with a flood of nausea, the horrible happenings in the Hotel Rhapsody Palas. After this lot, there'd be another next week. Why couldn't they all stay at home and have their holidays there?

'It's very nice of you to come,' she said to Joan and Joan.

'Are they looking after you properly, dear? Do you know what's the matter with you?'

'Shush! She mightn't want to tell us. Stop being nosey!'

Carly told them.

'I've never heard of that, have you, Joan? Does it hurt?'

'Of course it hurts, Joan.'

'Is there anything you'd like us to do for you, dear?'

'Take me home with you!' groaned Carly. 'I want to go home!'

'You mean England, dear?'

'Of course she means England, Joan. But you can't go back yet, dear. The season's not over. Indeed, it's not even August yet.'

Carly groaned again, and turned her face to the window, from where she could see a mass of dense red bougainvillaea against the usual blue sky. 'I don't think I'm very good at this job.' She'd suspected this for some time, but it had taken the shock of her illness to make her say it.

'Of course you are, dear. You mustn't let the hospital get

you down. I remember – do you remember when I was in Princess Beatrice with my leg, Joan? When was it, eighty-one or eighty-two?'

'It was in nineteen eighty.'

'Was it really? Well, I got very depressed, didn't I? I think it was the food. There seemed to be custard with everything.'

'It wasn't the food,' said Joan crisply, 'and anyway I brought you in a good many delicacies from M and S. You've forgotten that, haven't you? It wasn't the food, it was the smell, and because you were with all those sick people.'

'The smell,' reminisced Joan, 'and all that banging of metal instruments. But Miss Atkins doesn't want to hear about my experiences in the Princess Beatrice Hospital, do you, dear?'

'We bring you greetings from everyone in the Hotel Rhapsody Palas,' said Joan, which didn't help, either.

'Miss Atkins,' said Joan suddenly, 'there's a question Joan and I would like to ask you.'

'No, not now, Joan!' hissed Joan crossly.

'Would you say Mr Holbeach was a spy?'

Carly tried to focus her attention on Joan's question. The criss-cross of stitches up her stomach was pulling at her flesh, and something inside was hurting quite a lot as well. She moved slightly, hoping that a change of position would ease the pain. 'Ouch!'

'Shall we get a nurse, dear?'

Carly shook her head. 'The nasty one's on. She's got a moustache and she hates me because I'm not married.'

Joan looked at Joan, who also had a moustache. 'She means,' explained Joan, 'that it's against their religion for women to, well, consort with men outside marriage.'

'Oh yes. Well, what do you think about Mr Holbeach, dear?'

'I thought he was a writer.'

'He is, of sorts. But for a political magazine.' She pronounced 'political' as though it were a very difficult and unusual word.

'I don't know,' said Carly. 'He could be. They're a rum lot. But who would he be spying for?'

'We saw him,' said Joan excitedly, 'we saw him talking *Turkish* to soldiers, and we saw him once with a woman in a little bar up in the hills, didn't we, Joan? She was very glamorous,' continued Joan unabated. 'She had long reddish brown hair and black shiny high-heeled shoes with diamonds at the back.'

'Well, I don't suppose they were real diamonds,' observed Joan.

'No. As a matter of fact, I don't think the hair was real either. There was something rather, well, *mannish* about her, wasn't there, Joan?'

Carly considered. 'Well, it's none of our business, is it really?' This seemed the most satisfactory answer she could think of.

When Joan and Joan had gone, the nurse gave Carly a large injection of pethidine for the physical pain she was in. It took the edge off it, but allowed her to drift off into a cloud of emotional self-pity in which she felt too drained even to engage in the exercise of thinking about all the awful things she'd do to all the men she knew once she'd got her hands on them.

'Why is it,' said Dodo Delancey happily, back in the Hotel Rhapsody Palas, 'that men are incapable of packing properly?' She was commenting on the state of Crispin's suitcase, wherein clean clothes (the sweaters he didn't need and the smart light cotton suit she'd made him bring but there'd been no call for) lay loosely conjugated with the dirty ones: jeans striped with bicycle oil and factor twenty suntan cream, t-shirts redolent with sweat and streaked with aubergine and tomato and thick yellow olive oil, and in between the clothes the few books Crispin had brought but hadn't read, and his Walkman and Simon and Garfunkel and Mozart tapes, and his camera which he hadn't used, and the Proper Holidays brochure Dodo had also told him to bring in case the place wasn't up to scratch, and they needed to complain.

Three weeks was long enough. Dodo had got a good tan, and she was ready to go home to show it off. Losing a bit of weight through eating contaminated food in the carpet shop had been a bonus. She hadn't told Crispin yet about the rugs.

Crispin slunk away, leaving Dodo to pack properly. He edged back to the bar, where the sun was setting and Martin Holbeach was watching it morosely, cracking a bag of pistachio nuts.

'Dodo's packing,' he explained.

'Well, that's probably a good idea.'

'Time and place and circumstance,' said Martin slowly, 'but particularly place. They affect our behaviour, don't they, Delancey? You set a load of tourists down in a place like this, with the sun and the flowers and the history, and what do you get? A conflagration.'

'A conflagration,' Crispin repeated.

'Fire,' said Martin.

'I know. So it's all due to this place?'

'Not all of it. You need good material to start a fire. We all came here with the dry wood of our problems, our predicaments, our lack of understanding of ourselves and each other. We all left behind the ordinary structures that keep these things under control.'

Crispin looked at Martin curiously. 'Are you really a transvestite?'

'What's it to you if I am?'

'I just wondered.'

'Women are so much nicer than men, don't you think?' observed Martin obscurely.

'That's not what you said the other day.'

'I've never particularly admired consistency, either as a political or as a personal virtue. I'll tell you this, though, I think I've made up my mind about something.'

'You have?'

'I'm going to leave Sandy. It's not fair on the old girl. She'd be better off without me. So would Josh. It might help to solve all this Oedipal business she keeps going on about.'

Martin's voice broke with emotion. Crispin put a hand out to comfort him, and then withdrew it abruptly.

'It's all right, you can touch me. I haven't got AIDS like poor Barrett. That maid was right, though, wasn't she? Things are a mess. Not just here, but globally. The whole environmental system, politics. I suppose in view of that we ought to put the little buggers first more than we do.'

Crispin nodded. The sun went behind the rock tombs, not for the last time, but for the last time that the two of them would ever see in that place. He remembered scrambling up the rockface with Dodo and Star and Jade only the other day, though it seemed a long time ago. He thought of Dodo happily packing. He thought of Jade and Star probably less happily on their way back to the hotel. He thought of Tanza Road and Delancey Designs and the dream of Disney Stafford and the turtle that started all of this. 'I think I've decided something, too,' he said, more to himself than to Martin. He realized suddenly that his love for the goddess in the golden bikini had been only a diversion – it was like the sun rising and setting, a warm glow that could be gone almost as soon as it had begun. What is love, anyway, but a tension between the immanence of the present and the duties of past and future, calling to one another like the egrets and the spoonbills insistently over the great golden path of the sun? Life is for loving only to the permanent flower-children, or the crazy. The rest of the time, for the rest of us, there is only an endless cycle of labour and material accumulation – what Dodo calls 'responsibility'. It's because there are no eyeholes in all this labour through which the essential, forgotten splendour of being can even be glimpsed that we are so drawn to love. Love gives us a remembrance of what it is like to exist without all the complications of everyday consciousness. But love traps as well as frees. It has its own rules, its own bondage. All we do is exchange one form of oppression for another. 'I'll just have to struggle on, won't I?' said Crispin after a while out loud.

'Will you, old chap? Yes, you probably will.'

'And it probably won't be so bad, will it? The kids'll grow up, but that'll be all right. It'll be a relief really. They'll go away and lead their own lives and maybe they'll do it better than their parents have.'

Martin nodded. 'And we can get on with our own.'

'Whatever that means.'

The four motorbikes came over the mountains just after nine o'clock the following morning, and Jade and Star and Aaron and Kelly and Joshua were back in the Hotel Rhapsody Palas an hour later, having said goodbye to Yusuf and Celik and Tansil by the statue of the footballer in Karput. They exchanged addresses. Yusuf and Celik both wanted to see London one day, though Jade and Star weren't sure they ever wanted to see Karput again.

'Did we give you a shock, Mum?' asked Jade cheerfully.

Dodo's eyes glazed over. 'Are you all right, dear?'

'A bit tired and dirty, but otherwise, yes. And our virtues are still intact, just in case you were wondering about them. It's surprising what high moral principles some of today's youth have when you get to know them!'

'What do you mean, dear?'

'I'll tell you when you're older.'

'Didn't think I'd really keep them all over at the chrome mills till after the plane was supposed to have gone, didja?' said Joshua Holbeach to his father.

'How was I to know, Josh?'

'Are you all right, Dad?'

'That's a strange question coming from you.'

'I know about your little secret, Dad.'

'What secret?'

'Aw, come on, Dad!'

'Well, it's probably just as well. There's quite a lot to be sorted out, old man.'

'Sure. But you're not on your own, you know, Dad.' Joshua put out his hand to touch his father, and didn't withdraw it abruptly.

Father and son looked at each other in mutual amazement. Kelly Upton, on the other hand, didn't amaze either of her parents, and was full of the same bad language and obvious disrespect as she always had been. 'It's wonderful to have you back,' tried Lisa, attempting to be a good mother. 'Your father says we're going to try the Algarve next year. A villa with our own pool. You'd like that, wouldn't you?'

Aaron Shaw told *his* mother, who was sitting by the pool with Crispin, that he'd packed, and was going off with Star for a last look at the rock tombs.

'Okay, fine.' She turned her head to look at him, squinting in the sun. 'I'm just saying goodbye to Star's father.'

'We're all going back to England,' pointed out Aaron.

'You know what I mean.'

'Cool it! See you in a bit.' He strode off.

'Well,' Crispin got up, 'I must go and pay the bill.'

He settled down at the bar with a coffee. 'Not so busy today, Kizi?'

Kizi was drying glasses carefully with a large white towel. 'They are all packing their suitcases, Mr Delancey.'

'And finding out how much it's all cost them!'

'This hotel is good value,' insisted Kizi.

'I'm sure it is.'

Half an hour later Star Delancey and Aaron Shaw sat opposite the hotel in the rock tombs looking down on it all from a totally different perspective. They were perched on a rock – round them tourists climbed like clumsy goats – and they faced the sea, which joined the blue bowl of the sky on a hot misty horizon.

'Did you know Josh was writing a novel?' asked Star.

'How do you know?'

'Jade told me.'

'Well, I hope it's not about us.'

'No. What I don't understand,' said Star, after a silence, 'is why they complain about the crazy things we do all the time. We don't do any more than they do.'

'Especially when you consider that they're older and they've got all this experience they keep telling us about. They shouldn't need to do crazy things any more.'

'Is my dad going to go on seeing your mum?'

'No.'

'How do you know?'

'She told me.'

'Oh. That's good. I don't want to come from a broken home.'

'You mean like me?'

'No, Aaron, I'm sorry, I didn't mean that.'

'Don't worry, it's not broken. There was nothing to break. My father didn't want to know me, apparently. You're lucky – at least you've got a father, even if he is a bit of a handful sometimes.'

'Are *we* going to see each other again after today?'

'I hope so. I'd like to.'

'So would I.'

'That's all right, then.'

Star and Aaron came down from the rock tombs. 'The bus will be here at three o'clock,' said Mehmet firmly. He didn't want to lose any of them again.

The two Joans have bought Carly a get well card which they give to Mehmet to deliver. Portia has put all the Mills & Boons back, and Lisa Upton and Sandy Holbeach and Dodo Delancey have all been separately into Karput to make last minute purchases of holiday presents: thin silver jewellery, painted plates, and leather bum bags, but no more carpets. Wilma Blake comes out of her room just as the Proper Holidays bus draws up. She has her folded raincoat over her arm, ready for the English weather, and yesterday's *Daily Mail* to read on the plane. She's given the maid, Bilge, an envelope with a £50 note in it. She'd pressed it into Bilge's hand: 'You'll have to change it somewhere, but I'm sure you'll be able to make good use of it. I wish I could speak your language. We could have had a proper talk, then.'

The bus takes them out of Karput for the last time. The town waits there for them, in the curve of the reed-edged river, with its low-slung hotels and its cafés offering poorly spelt food, and its shops selling turtle t-shirts and sham Gucci jackets and over-priced Ambre Solaire, and its tourist office showing endless repeats of baby turtles being born and striking out towards the moonlit sea. On the river, the blue and white boats ply back and forth with equal repetitiveness up to the black odoriferous mud baths and down to the sweeping sands of the Aegean Sea. The tourists on the bus see Karput, and they see the river, and they know where it goes, for they have all been there. They have sampled all the attractions of the area; they have been and done what the Proper Holidays brochure told them they should do. They have looked, and they have bathed and they have eaten and they have drunk, and then they have looked again to make sure that they have really seen and done what they thought they were supposed to.

On the bus, Crispin sits next to Dodo and behind Meg Shaw. He studies the back of Meg's crinkly hair intently until he finds Dodo looking at him, and then he watches the flat burnt green landscape passing the window. As he had done on their way from the airport, the driver points out the trees where the storks nest, and where two of them can, indeed, be seen now, in their most unlikely postures. Just before the airport, a dreadful woman with a Colgate smile and blood-red lips on a large hoarding advertising Sultan Air urges Crispin to Fly and Smile. Dodo is chattering away beside him. 'I think it'd be nice to have a party when we get back, don't you? Just a few friends. It's time we did that. Are you listening, Crispin?'

When they've passed through the military gate at the airport, Roger from Proper Holidays, Carly's substitute, smiles at them, like the woman in the Sultan Air advertisement. 'Isn't he the young man who . . . ?' whispered Joan to Joan.

'Shush! Miss Atkins wouldn't want everyone to know!'

Jade and Star are clattering around the concourse in their boots. 'I expect the flight'll be delayed,' says Crispin mournfully.

Lisa Upton makes a fuss because they've been put in smoking seats. 'My daughter has asthma,' she lies, 'it could be fatal.'

'Oh shut up, Mum,' says Kelly, 'all my friends smoke anyway.'

Crispin is next to Ronald Dunkerley in the checking-in queue. 'You had a good holiday, then?' asks Ronald.

'I suppose. At least it's been a change. What about you?'

'It's been interesting.' That's what Ronald will say in the staff common room to Perkins, whose fault it was that they came here in the first place. Yes, it certainly was an interesting place you sent us to, Perkins. 'Why did you come here, Delancey?'

'A friend told us about it. My wife says she needs to go somewhere sunny every year. We couldn't go anywhere too pricey. My work's okay, but it *is* the recession.'

'You see, it's all a question of accident,' observes Ronald, checking the labels on their suitcases. He looks thoughtfully down the airport concourse. 'That's what history is, a series of accidents. You came here because a friend suggested it. We came here because a colleague of mine recommended the fluted columns at Punka. Gareth Barrett came here because the Cardiff branch of the European Bird-watching Society spotted that Karput is on the migratory path of the lemon-breasted whatever it is. The Uptons came because they couldn't afford Sorrento again. The Holbeaches, well we don't really know about their motives, do we?'

Their bags are X-rayed and their passports examined and then they are processed through to the duty-free hall where the prices of everything are a good deal more than they'd pay back home. The plane is only an hour late taking off. On it, Crispin reaches in his bag for the dog-eared copy of *Dracula* Meg Shaw gave him as a parting present. On his left, daughter Star frowns at his choice of reading matter. On his right, daughter Jade studies the plastic card of instructions about how to escape from the plane.

He opens the book, and is soon deep in the details of someone else's journey from west to east, a journey that was considerably more melodramatic than the one he has made, but which was just as replete with historical accidents and with moral messages, being all about the vanquishing of wrong by right, the proper roles of men and women, and the correct identification and rooting out of evil in all its forms.